Dedalus Original Fiction in Paperback

Codename Xenophon

Leo Kanaris is a teacher in southern Greece.

Codename Xenophon is his first novel. He is currently writing a
sequel *Blood & Gold*

This is a work of fiction.
Occasional references to historical events, characters
and places are used for fictional purposes.

Leo Kanaris

Codename Xenophon

Dedalus

Supported using public funding by
**ARTS COUNCIL
ENGLAND**

Published in the UK by Dedalus Limited,
24-26, St Judith's Lane, Sawtry, Cambs, PE28 5XE
email: info@dedalusbooks.com
www.dedalusbooks.com

ISBN printed book 978 1 909232 83 9
ISBN ebook 978 1 910213 01 8

Dedalus is distributed in the USA by SCB Distributors,
15608 South New Century Drive, Gardena, CA 90248
email: info@scbdistributors.com   web: www.scbdistributors.com

Dedalus is distributed in Australia by Peribo Pty Ltd.
58, Beaumont Road, Mount Kuring-gai, N.S.W. 2080
email: info@peribo.com.au

First published by Dedalus in 2014
Codename Xenophon copyright © Leo Kanaris 2014

The right of Leo Kanaris to be identified as the author of this work has been
asserted by him in accordance with the Copyright, Designs and Patents Act,
1988.

Printed in Finland by Bookwell
Typeset by Marie Lane

1

Like much of the city around it, 43 Aristotle Street had seen better days. The marble steps, the smoked-glass doors, the rows of dark wooden mailboxes, all had a dowdy, dreary, superannuated feel. Two cement plant tubs stood side by side in the lobby. One held a struggling jasmine, kept alive by an old lady on the ground floor. The other, empty and dry, had survived by default, an ugly ornament that no one could be bothered to throw away.

Returning home from a trip out of town, George Zafiris felt the tiredness of the building as part of his own. The door creaked shut behind him. Although the day was bright, it was dark in here. He pressed the light switch and one low-energy bulb, its white tubes poking like the legs of a trapped insect out of a spotlight on the wall, began to glow feebly. A musty smell enveloped him: of damp, disinfectant and old soup. He was not a gloomy man, but the thought flashed through his mind, as it sometimes had before, that this was a lobby to shoot yourself in.

He unlocked his mailbox and gathered its contents, glancing at the envelopes as he climbed the stairs. One handwritten, the rest bills and rubbishy advertising.

At the top of the stairs he turned the key in the lock. Three, four times, the bolts clanking and echoing in the marble stairwell. He walked in, leaving the door ajar, and dropped the leaflets in the bin. The place felt dusty and close, even after two days away. He moved from room to room, hauling up roller blinds, flinging wide the windows. The light pounced in, dazzling and hot.

The letter was a proper one, with a stamp and a handwritten address. Good quality paper. He opened a drawer, moved aside a tin of ammunition, a Beretta 950B Jetfire pistol, a summons to appear in court for shouting at a policeman, some notes on mental relaxation, a long-range microphone, and a framed photograph of his wife on a beach in 1992, the glass cracked in one corner. Under them all lay a Bechtold & Schmidt 'Predator' flick-knife, a lethal memento of a long-concluded investigation. He kept it there, honed and oiled, just in case. He opened the knife and slid its blade under the flap of the envelope.

A voice from the doorway made him look up.

'Mr George?'

Dimitri from the café downstairs stood holding an aluminium tray with a tripod-shaped hanger.

'Shall I bring it in there?'

'Thank you.'

George took a euro coin from his pocket.

'How was the trip?' asked Dimitri.

George took a sip of coffee. 'I don't enjoy funerals,' he said. 'They make me feel old before my time.'

Dimitri pronounced the traditional formula: 'May you live to remember your friend.'

George nodded. His mind was flooded with images, his heart with loss.

'I just want my old friend back, for one more lunch together.

One more ouzo by the sea.'

Dimitri seemed to feel his sorrow. 'I know the feeling,' he said, 'it doesn't seem much to ask. A moment, that's all. But you'll never get it. That's for sure.'

George knew Dimitri was thinking of his wife. She was still alive, just, but on borrowed time.

'How's Tasia?' asked George.

'The same,' said Dimitri.

'No news, good or bad?'

'Just waiting.'

'Give her a kiss from me. Tell her to get well.'

'I will,' said Dimitri and left him, closing the door gently.

George picked up the envelope again. The address was in black: a neat, educated script. Postmark Aegina. He unfolded a single sheet of notepaper.

> *Dear Mr Zafiris,*
>
> *I was given your name by a business associate, who described you as reliable and moderate in your fees. I may have occasion to hire you. A member of my family has been murdered. The police have made no progress with the case. I need someone to investigate this thoroughly and with absolute discretion. Telephone me as soon as you receive this.*
>
> *Constantine Petrakis*

The name made him stop and think. He didn't know the man personally, but this was a historic family. A dynasty even. Lawyers, politicians, intellectuals. Before that, warlords, heroes of 1821. When the call to arms came, they had summoned their supporters from villages and sheepfolds across the mountains of the Peloponnese, and chased the hated Ottomans from the land. There was a Petrakis Street in every town in Greece.

He checked his watch. It was four thirty. No point calling for at least two hours. Petrakis would be asleep. That would get everything off to a bad start. He pushed the letter aside. Feeling drowsy despite the coffee, he lay down on his day-bed and closed his eyes.

*

He slept badly, fighting off a crowd of memories. An island port, the ferry approaching through sharp morning light. The ramp descending, a hearse rolling out. His old friend Mario inside, 47 years old. On the jetty, next to the whitewashed café, the dead man's wife Eleni and their two sons. Waiting, still as statues. Their faces blank, even when George greeted them, as if they had lost the power to move.

Then the procession, slow and reluctant, up the hill to the church.

At six he woke up, feeling drugged and heavy. He staggered into the shower and let the cold spray startle him awake.

With a towel round his waist he poured a beer from the fridge, settled on the sofa, and dialled the number in Aegina.

Constantine Petrakis had a tense, dry voice, with the grating quality of a door on rusty hinges.

'I only know the bare facts, Mr Zafiris. My brother was shot here on the island. You must speak to the lady who found him. Only she won't use the telephone, you must see her face to face. And her house is tricky to find. I'll have to show you, there's no other way. John was staying with her. He often visited. Why anyone would wish to shoot him is beyond me.

He was an eminent man, with a worldwide reputation. And the police are pathetic. Bureaucrats, every one of them. They specialise in doing nothing. Tell me, when can you come?'

George glanced at his diary, which was empty for the whole week.

'Tomorrow morning? Eleven o'clock?'

'Perfect. I'll see you at the Hotel Brown. Do you know it?'

'I'll find it.'

2

George lived apart from his wife for most of the year. It was not an arrangement he liked, but he accepted it as a compromise. It had its roots in dark times. If he dwelt on those he would really get depressed, but he chose not to. From early spring to late autumn Zoe stayed in Andros, at her father's village house, painting, writing poetry, looking after the garden and a collection of aunts and eccentric cousins. Meanwhile George toiled away in Athens, visiting the island for rare weekends and – with luck – a fortnight every August. In winter she would join him in the city, and they would have a more conventional married life. Their son Nick was studying engineering in Newcastle; a safe profession, they hoped, for unsafe times.

George's working days, like everyone's in Athens, were complicated. Cases were opened, pursued, baulked, interrupted. New ones appeared. Clients went silent, or vanished. Some had to be investigated in their turn. Either they'd run out of money or got tangled up in complications of their own. The national crisis didn't help. Businesses were going bust, salaries and pensions shrinking with horrible speed. People were getting ill, going mad, wanting to disappear from their own lives.

'Ade na vris ákri.' The phrase was on everyone's lips. 'You don't know where to begin.'

George was lucky. He had no outstanding loans, and no one owed him money. Not serious money, at least. But work was falling off. Only the rich could afford to pay, and even they were being careful these days. He took any offer that came his way.

The voice of Petrakis had filled him with mistrust. Not what he said, just the way he said it. After some expensive mistakes, he had developed an instinct for difficult characters. This was one to be wary of.

George stood on the deck of the *Aghios Nektarios* in Piraeus, enjoying the breeze and the widening gap of water between him and the city. Slowly but steadily the tangle of urban sensations left him. The horizon blossomed with mountains, outlined sharp as metal cut-outs against a silvery-blue sky. Gulls rode the ship's slipstream, their wings unmoving, only their heads tilting side to side in the search for food.

They passed through a strange ocean landscape of laid-up tankers and cargo ships. Images of a stalled economy, going nowhere. Waiting. Once in a while a powerboat surged by, slicing open the blue surface of the sea with a brilliant white trail of foam. At the helm a middle-aged man – big belly, shades, gold neck-chain and bracelet – accompanied inevitably by a girl in a bikini, half his age, probably eastern European. In the back seat, a bored Alsatian dog. The market had crashed two years ago, but luxury – of this strange, 1960s, cigarette advertisement kind – still flourished. Like the cafés of downtown Athens, packed with people paying monstrous prices for their iced cappuccinos while they complained about the crisis.

After an hour they reached Aegina. The anchors rattled down and the ferry backed onto the jetty in a cloud of diesel exhaust. A voice on the public address system, urgent and harsh, told passengers to get off at once: 'the ship will depart immediately.'

The Hotel Brown stood a few hundred metres away, at the far end of the waterfront. George strolled past fishing boats, fruit-stalls, cafés, a kiosk hung with glossy magazines and plastic toys. With ten minutes still to spare, he sat in a dusty church garden where a bust of Kapodistria – first prime minister of Greece, gunned down in his fifties by a political opponent – stared out from a ring of palm trees at the sea.

Petrakis was lean, precise, seventy years old. A nervous light flickered in his pale green eyes. His shoes, trousers and shirt were expensively elegant, his watch a piece of Swiss real estate. He shook hands quickly, without warmth.

'We'll sit in the garden.'

Petrakis led him to a table under a loquat tree and irritably brushed three fallen leaves from his chair before sitting down. He examined his visitor for a moment before speaking.

'Let me give you some information about my brother. After that I shall take you to meet Madame Corneille. It was in her apartment that the tragedy occurred.'

'I've kept the whole day free,' said George.

'We won't need that long. The facts are straightforward. My brother was a classical scholar. He taught at Stanford, Princeton, and latterly King's College, London. He was a man of outspoken – even controversial – views. He did early work on Plato, but he was best known for his writings on the less palatable aspects of ancient Greek life. What he called 'the darkness behind the light'. Slavery, prostitution, crime and punishment, paedophilia, homosexuality, and, I very much regret to say, even child sacrifice, although the evidence for that is circumstantial. You can imagine how such work was received here, especially in patriotic circles.'

George nodded.

'John was about to give a lecture on this entirely unsuitable subject to the Aegina Historical Society. This was arranged by Madame Corneille, in association with local friends, for nine o'clock on the evening of March 25th.'

Petrakis paused, waiting for a reaction.

'Go on,' said George.

'I expect you to note the significance of the date.'

'It may be significant or not.'

'It can only be significant!'

'We mustn't jump to conclusions.'

Petrakis seemed irritated. 'As you please, Mr Zafiris. I ask you merely to be aware that my brother was shot on the day when we celebrate our national independence.'

'I note that fact,' said George. He met the man's agitated stare calmly. 'Go on.'

'At about seven, John went for a shower. He never came out. Half an hour later, Madame Corneille knocked, got no answer, entered the bathroom, and found him. He had been shot in the head. She summoned the police at once; and there, I am sorry to say, the matter has languished.'

George thought about it while the waiter served coffee.

'Tell me some more about your brother.'

'There's nothing more to tell.'

'There has to be.'

'Nothing else of relevance.'

'I need to know about his private life.'

'There's nothing to hide.'

'Maybe not, but I need to know.'

Again the irritated look. 'What exactly do you need to know?'

'His relationship with Madame Corneille for a start.'

'Above suspicion!'

13

'Other people on the island?'

'A few friends. Trusted people.'

'I'll need their names.'

'Not relevant.'

'It may be highly relevant.'

'I can assure you it's not.'

'I'll make up my own mind about that.'

'I am trying to save you time. Which of course means money for me. I presume you charge by the hour, by the way, like a lawyer?'

'I do, but nothing like a lawyer's rates.'

Petrakis looked sceptical. 'What is your rate, if I may ask?'

'Basic is 50 an hour, plus expenses.'

'How long do such jobs normally take?'

'Impossible to say.'

'Why?'

'Some go quickly, others drag on for months.'

'I want this one to go quickly.'

'So do I.'

Petrakis grimaced. He sipped his coffee as if it might be poisoned.

'What else do you need to know, Mr Zafiris?'

'I've told you. His personal life. That's where the answers usually lie.'

'In his case, I doubt it.'

'Very well.' George drained his cup. 'I'll send my bill for this morning's visit.'

'We have to see Madame Corneille!'

George stood up. 'You go and see her. I'm wasting my time.'

Petrakis said calmly, 'You are very impatient.'

'I have other cases to attend to.'

'You said you had the whole day free.'

14

'For work. Not for sitting around.'

'Calm down, Mr Zafiris!'

'I'm perfectly calm. Either you give me more information or I leave.'

'Very well.' Petrakis raised his hands from the table. 'My brother was a homosexual. Is that what you want to know?'

George said coldly, 'It may be. It may not be. I need to know more.'

'I don't see why!'

'Did he get mixed up with people who provide certain services, or indulge certain tastes, perhaps unpalatable ones to use your word?'

'I don't know what you mean.'

'Strangling, asphyxia, bondage? Things go wrong sometimes. Accidents, crazy partners. Criminals…'

'I can assure you he was not that type.'

'Do you know that for certain?'

'He never mentioned anything of the kind!'

'Did you talk about it with him?'

'Absolutely not!'

'All right,' said George. 'Let's go back to basics. How do you know he was gay?'

'He had a "partner" as they say.' Petrakis spoke with disdain.

'What sort of a partner?'

A long, pained look. 'Not the sort of man you would expect around a professor of ancient history.'

'Well?'

'A builder. And decorator. Of a sort.'

'Where was this partner when John was killed?'

'On a flight to London.'

'I'll need to talk to him.'

Petrakis's irritation spilled over again. 'If any of this gets out to the press, I will personally –'

'It won't.'

Petrakis was silent for a few moments. 'All right. I'll give you Bill's number when I'm back in Athens.'

'Thank you. Now tell me about John's relationship with Madame Corneille. And please stick to what you know.'

'She was purely a friend and admirer.'

'That sounds a little bland.'

'She's an eccentric. A spiritualist. A psychic healer.'

'Did he consult her professionally?'

'I have no idea.'

'What did he say about her?'

'Very little. She was just a friend.'

'Did he have enemies?'

'Hundreds! His books caused great anger.'

'How was that expressed?'

'Letters, articles in the press, attacks on television and radio. Luckily, none of these people knew anything of his private life. If they had, he would never have been left in peace.'

'Is there anyone here in Aegina who was particularly upset by his writings?'

'I could suggest a name or two.'

'OK. That needs looking into. Now, the police. Who have you been dealing with? Locals, or someone from Athens?'

'Locals as far as I know. The investigation seems to be in the hands of a certain Captain Bagatzounis. A ridiculous man!'

'What has he done?'

'Nothing! That is my problem! This man has done nothing at all!'

George had heard this complaint many times before. 'With respect, Mr Petrakis, even a Greek police inspector can't do nothing when faced with a murder.'

Petrakis spluttered, 'Of course he did the minimum! The bureaucratic minimum. Took statements and photographs, strutted around the apartment, glanced out of the window, asked a few utterly obvious questions. He may even have compiled a report. But effectively he has done nothing!'

'Is GADA involved?'

'GADA?'

'The central police authority.'

'I don't know. They give out no information. Certainly not to me! Every inquiry is met with blankness and evasion. They are incredible. In a modern democracy, to behave with such contempt for the public!'

George said nothing. There was something hollow in this man's words.

Petrakis glanced at his watch. 'We must go to Madame Corneille. She will be waiting. Are you ready?'

3

They walked up a lane of low 19th-century houses, overhung with fig trees. The pavement was narrow, a broken strip of concrete obstructed by rubbish bins, pallets of bricks and badly parked scooters. They had to step into the roadway, squeezing against a wall when a car came by, filling the lane with exhaust.

They turned into a street of shops, lively with mid-morning conversations. A butcher, an ironmonger, a baker. Past the cathedral, with its ochre-painted bell tower and nesting doves. Past a ruined mansion, windows and roof open to the sky. They came to an alley of dazzling white houses and courtyards, draped with laundry drying in the fierce sun. They climbed a flight of steps. Petrakis pressed the bell.

The door was opened by a woman in her forties, slim, lithe, in an open-necked white shirt and blue jeans. Her eyes, a deep grey-blue, were set in a pale and pensive face, with a halo of frizzy golden hair.

'Constantine! My darling! Welcome.'

'This is the gentleman I told you about, Rosa. Mr George Zafiris.'

They shook hands. George was struck by the softness of her skin, her otherworldly air.

The entrance hall was shuttered, dark and cool. A smoke-trail of incense hung sweetly in the gloom. She led them into the lounge, lit by a single ray of intense light that cut through a gap in the wooden shutters and lay across the floor like a strip of gold.

'Your aura is down, Costa,' she said, turning on Petrakis without preamble. 'You need to look after yourself.'

'Are you surprised?' said Petrakis angrily.

'Not in the least. But this is the time for repair. For healing.' She glanced at George.

'There you see a man with an excellent aura!'

'Pleased to hear it,' said George.

'Look at his shoulders. Strong but relaxed. Yours are hunched, like a gnome. A goblin. You're much too nervous.'

'Let's leave all that,' said Petrakis. 'We're here on business.'

'Fine. You do your business, I'll do mine. Sit down, gentlemen.'

They each took a chair. George's eyes were getting used to the half-light.

'I need to ask you about the shooting of John Petrakis,' he said.

She lit a cigarette. 'I hope this doesn't bother you.' She waved the smoke vaguely away. 'It was a horrible experience for me.'

'Of course.'

'John was a close friend. We had a consonance of intellect, of artistic interests, of feeling. He was a genius, A companion soul. We were not lovers, although I sensed very strongly that in another life we might have been. Often we lead many lives, in parallel…'

Petrakis cut in. 'Just tell Mr Zafiris what happened.'

'I'm coming to it, in my own time. This is not easy.'

'Tell it your way,' said George.

'On the evening of his lecture he went into the shower, just after seven o'clock. We had been listening to the BBC news.

He took his towel, his shampoo, his bath bag. He said *I shan't be long*. But at half-past seven I noticed that he still hadn't come out. I was worried. I knocked, I waited, I knocked again. I could hear the shower still running, which was odd. John was a spartan type, he never wasted water. So I called his name. There was no reply. I called again. Silence... I had a terrible misgiving. I opened the door and there...' She stopped, her voice catching. Tears began running down her cheeks. She took a deep breath.

'You heard no shot?'

She shook her head.

'Can you tell me what you saw?'

'He was hanging over the side of the bathtub, limp as a piece of cloth, with blood...' – her hands waved in circles – '...sprayed everywhere.'

George waited.

'That's it,' she said hopelessly. 'I called the doctor who lives round the corner. He listened for a heartbeat. Nothing. He was gone. Then we called the police. They invaded my flat, treated me first as a suspect, then as a nuisance, and then lost interest in the case.'

'What were you doing for the half hour that the professor was in the shower?'

'I was getting dressed.'

'And you heard nothing?'

'I was listening to music.'

'Loud music?'

'Not especially. But my bedroom door was shut, so was the bathroom...'

'Was there anything in the hours or days leading up to the murder that seemed unusual? Any incidents? Odd remarks?'

'Nothing. This was lightning from a clear sky.'

'OK. Is there anybody, either here or in Athens, who had a reason to kill the professor?'

'No. He was admired and respected by all who knew him.'

'He upset people with his books.'

'Of course! Bigots, fanatical patriots.'

'Is it possible they knew where he was staying?'

'Most unlikely.'

'Did anyone else know he was here?'

'A couple of friends.'

'Did they meet him?'

'We had dinner together the night before he died.'

'Here, or out?'

Petrakis interrupted. 'I can't see what –'

'Hush, dear Costa! It's a reasonable question. If we were out, our conversation could well have been overheard. Is that not what you were interested to know, Mr Zafiris?'

'My thinking precisely.'

'We dined here.'

'I may have to speak to your friends.'

'Of course. Their names are Abbas and Camilla. Telephone number 58360.'

George made a note. 'I now have a question of a more personal nature.'

'Feel free.'

'Did the professor have any sexual adventures during his stay?'

She glanced at Petrakis, who said wearily, 'He knows about Bill.'

'Bill was with him until the morning of the lecture,' she said. 'Then he flew back to London. But I would not call Bill a "sexual adventure". They were practically married.'

'Why didn't he stay for the lecture?'

'He wouldn't have understood it,' said Petrakis.

'Nonsense! He would have understood it perfectly. Bill had work in London the next day.'

'Was there any sign of tension between them?'

She thought about this. 'No. They were relaxed.'

'What sort of man is Bill?'

'A good man, intelligent, practical, with a certain aesthetic development, but of course he's imprisoned by a materialist vision of existence, as you would expect of a builder.'

'What do you mean by that?'

'He sees only the physical. No spiritual dimension whatsoever.'

'To say the least!' said Petrakis.

'Costa! Control your snobbery!'

'Did you ever see them argue?' asked George.

'Only in play. "You've stolen my sun cream" – that kind of thing.'

'Did John ever go out looking for rough trade?'

'I wouldn't know.'

'Did he meet anyone else here? Friends, associates, colleagues?'

'If he did, he never told me about it.'

'OK,' said George. 'As far as you know, nobody had any reason to kill him?'

'That's right. I find it impossible to believe that such a mild, harmless man, so open and amusing and cultivated, should have even one enemy.'

'I believe you're wrong, Rosa,' said Petrakis abruptly.

'OK, I'm wrong. You tell him your theory, Costa.'

'No,' said Petrakis sharply. 'This is not the moment. I want Mr Zafiris to reach his own conclusions. If he has eyes to see, let him see!'

'Fair enough,' said George.

'Any more questions, Mr Zafiris?'

'I'll need a list of contacts. The Chief of Police, the President of the Historical Society, everyone. And I need to see the bathroom.'

'Will you show him, Costa? I don't think I can bear it.'

'I'd prefer it if you show me yourself.'

'Why?' Petrakis objected.

George tried to be patient. 'Madame Corneille is the main witness. Her account of the crime is important.'

'She has already told you what she saw and heard.'

'I know.'

'So? What is the point of forcing the poor lady to go through it all again?'

'People often remember details at the scene of the crime. Subconscious recall, triggered by the senses. These details can be crucial. I don't ask Madame Corneille to do this lightly.'

'Facts are facts!'

'Facts are surprisingly slippery things.'

'Are you an investigator or an amateur philosopher, Mr Zafiris?'

'I just want to see the bathroom.'

'I think you've made that clear!'

'If you don't want me to do this job properly I'll go back to Athens and drop the case.'

'You've used that threat before.'

'Don't force me to use it again.'

Petrakis seethed. He was a man who had to be in control. George had met hundreds like him, all convinced they were unique; domestic dictators, forged in their mothers' worship of their sons. He waited for the counterstroke.

'I am not in the habit of paying for insolence, Mr Zafiris. I can get it any day I want for free.'

'I'm sure you can.'

'What's that supposed to mean?'

George stood up. 'Shall we stop wasting time?'

Petrakis waved a dismissive hand. 'Go with him, Rosa. Tell him what he wants to know. And try not to be too emotional.'

Madame Corneille closed her eyes, gathering herself.

They walked into a little vestibule hung with Indian and Persian prints. To the left a kitchen, to the right a pair of bedrooms. With a reluctant gesture she indicated the half-open bathroom door. George gently pushed it back. There was the bath under the window, the shower on the wall. He took off his shoes and stood in the bath. From there he saw what John Petrakis would have seen in the last few seconds of his life. Outside the window, directly opposite, a large neoclassical house in a well-ordered garden; beyond it, a jumbled townscape of alleys, houses, electrical cables and trees. With a rifle he could have shot into the windows of fifteen, maybe twenty homes. A gunman, he thought, might also risk firing from a rooftop or a courtyard. Probably not from the street.

'Whose is the big house opposite?' he asked.

'Colonel Varzalis.'

'Who's he?'

'A retired army officer.'

'It's ideally placed.'

'I know,' she said.

He watched her face, which was anxious and pained.

'Would you mind telling me exactly what you saw when you found the professor?'

She pointed to the bath. 'He was hanging over. Arms and head on the floor.'

'Can you remember his head?'

She shuddered. 'Of course. Half of it was missing.'

'And where were the fragments, the blood?'

'On the floor.'

'Anywhere else?'

'The shower curtain.'

'Where? Can you show me?'

'At the top. And running down.'

'Was it this shower curtain?'

'No. The police took it away.'

'Did they take anything else?'

'The bathmat. John's clothes and belongings.'

'Papers, wallet, passport?'

'Everything.'

'Do they still have them?'

'I have no idea.'

His eyes travelled around the bathroom once more. It was crowded with cosmetics and decorative objects. Everything was impeccably clean and orderly.

'You must have had a hell of a job clearing up,' he said.

She nodded. 'A whole day. On my knees, and up the ladder. Bleach, water and blood… There's no cleaning product in the world that can purge that image from my mind.'

4

Back at his desk in Athens that afternoon, George had an urgent matter to deal with. It had been on his books for a while. He called it his 'dirty political quartet'. A government minister, Byron Kakridis, had approached him in early May with a straightforward commission: to report on his wife's social life. It had not taken long to find out that she was having an out-of-hours romance with an opposition politician, Angelos Boiatzis. They met in a downtown hotel, once or twice a week, in a calm and settled routine which appeared not to harm anyone. George had been about to present his report when an intuition held him back. He never liked exposing extra-marital affairs, which often seemed justified by the misery of the marriage. Despite money, big cars and luxurious homes, these people were trapped in wretched lives, seeking freedom wherever they could find it.

He had been through all this himself, and wished now he had never known what his wife had been up to. The knowledge had poisoned him, burnt up his heart, destroyed his happiness… What good was achieved by proof?

In the case of Kakridis and Boiatzis, his usual hesitation was accompanied by a more shadowy sensation, a premonition of stranger things to come.

A few days later, a call came from Mrs Kakridis. Suddenly the woman he had been following and photographing for a month was asking him to follow her husband.

'I think he's having an affair,' she said.

He should have refused the case, but the old radical in him stirred. He could not resist the temptation to see what another of the nation's elected representatives was doing in his spare time. Torn between curiosity and professional correctness, he gave Mrs Kakridis the number of a fellow investigator, Hector Pezas. He and Hector shared information. It was hardly the most ethical arrangement in the world, but it worked.

Byron Kakridis was trickier to follow than his wife. He had a constituency in the north of the country. His life passed in a blizzard of flights, car journeys, meetings and sessions of parliament. Between these he was either on the telephone or asleep. Meals were snatched in unscheduled moments. The reading and drafting of papers could only have taken place late at night or early in the morning, at home or in hotel rooms. Hector Pezas came to the conclusion that this man could not possibly be having an affair.

He put this to Margarita Kakridis. She insisted. Her husband was a highly sexed man – 'a volcano', as she put it. He had lost interest in her too suddenly. There could only be one explanation. They stepped up the level of vigilance to 24 hours a day, with two extra investigators. George advised Pezas to take the money in advance. She paid, no hesitation. And Pezas, a thorough and conscientious man, finally got a result. Mr Kakridis used to slip out of parliamentary sittings using a back entrance, then walk to a flat in Pangrati, where he and an attractive blonde lady spent exactly forty-five minutes together behind closed doors. He would leave the flat and be back in his seat in the chamber in just under an hour. Not a hair out of place.

'Any idea who the blonde might be?' asked George.
'Yes.'

'Can you tell me?'

'It would be unethical.'

'Of course. But helpful.'

'All right. It's Mrs Boiatzis.'

'Mrs Boiatzis? Isn't she bit old for a goat like him?'

'You should see her. She's a hot thirty-five year old from Russia. I don't know where he found her, or she found him, but I tell you she's a hell of a woman.'

'So why is Boiatzis messing around with someone else?'

'Maybe the Russian's hard work. They usually are.'

Now they had to decide how to tell the truth to Mr and Mrs Kakridis. They went over the possibilities several times. Pezas saw it very simply. 'They've paid us for the information. It's our job to give it to them. What they do with it is their business.'

'I don't like what happens next,' said George. 'There's an equilibrium here. We're going to destroy it.'

'They've asked us to.'

'They don't know what they're doing.'

'They'll know soon enough.'

'They'll regret it.'

'That's their problem.'

'Can we at least send them a written report with a recommendation that they don't read it?'

'You're joking!'

'I'm not.'

'You'll only whet their appetite.'

'At least they'll have a warning.'

'Whatever you like. My report will be ready tomorrow.'

'I need a few more days.'

'Why?'

'I have to go to a friend's funeral tomorrow.'

'So I'll send mine.'

'Can't you wait, and we report simultaneously?'

'Why?'

'It's only fair. Three days is all I need.'

'OK. Friday seven p.m. and no going back.'

It was now five p.m. on Friday. George opened the file.

There were the daily registers of movements, the telephone numbers used by Mrs Kakridis, the recordings, the photographs, the envelope of receipts. With misgivings in his heart he switched on his laptop and drafted a summary of his findings.

It was a quick job. He had done it dozens of times before and the sentences flowed readily. "The subject was observed for a period of twenty-one days. On three occasions she visited the Hotel Socrates in Kotzias Street, spending two hours there each time. Her visits coincided with those of a well-dressed professional man who had booked a room under the name 'Karouzos'. A waiter took whisky and coffee to the room on each of their visits, noting that Mr Karouzos came to the door in a kimono on two occasions, and the subject herself, wrapped in a sheet, on one. No incriminating photography was possible as the room was curtained, but we were able to obtain a few pictures of Mr Karouzos and the subject sharing a cigarette at an open window. The evidence suggests an intimate relationship. No other activities or visits by the subject give rise to suspicions of any kind." He left it at that.

It was six forty-five. He telephoned Pezas.

'Are you ready?'

'Ready!'

'Warning first. Then, if they insist, the evidence to be sent by courier?'

'Agreed.'

He ended the call and dialled Mr Kakridis on his private line.

A harsh, impatient voice answered, setting his nerves on edge. George forced himself to stay calm. He told Kakridis that his suspicions were confirmed, and advised him not to pursue the case any further, or to examine the evidence, which would only upset him.

Kakridis exploded: 'You think I'm paying you to give me advice? And make unsupported allegations? You must be crazy!'

'These are not unsupported allegations, Mr Kakridis. I have all the proof you need.'

'Then show me, goddamn it!'

'I am recommending that you don't look at it.'

'Why?'

'For your own peace of mind.'

'Let me worry about my peace of mind! Just do your job and hand over the evidence.'

'You'll get the evidence. I'm just telling you...'

'Don't tell me anything!'

'OK, I won't.'

'If my wife's cheating on me, I need details.'

'It's a recipe for disaster.'

'She should have thought of that before she started.'

'The other thing to consider,' George continued patiently, 'is your own conduct.'

'What the hell are you talking about?'

'If you're going to make accusations, be sure you're without blame yourself.'

'Listen, friend, I don't need your lectures!'

'This is a warning I give all my clients.'

'Then you should be a priest, not a fucking detective.'

'I'll bear it in mind.'

'Get those documents to me at once.'

'I'll send a courier. Home or office?'

'Office! Mark it "strictly private and confidential" or my idiot secretary will open it and the whole bloody disaster will be in the papers by morning.'

George replaced the telephone. He sealed the envelope and rang a motorcycle courier. Then he closed his eyes.

The door-bell woke him. He checked the videophone. A man in motorcycle gear, his helmet under his arm, had come for the package.

'Second floor,' he said, and pressed the buzzer.

George poured himself a whisky and soda, thinking of 'Mr Karouzos' in the Hotel Socrates. Karouzos, indeed! As if he was some kind of opera singer!

He telephoned Pezas.

'How did you get on?'

'As expected,' said his colleague. 'She wanted the evidence.'

'You advised against it?'

'I did.'

'And?'

'She hit the roof.'

'Funny. Her husband did the same.'

'You see?' said Pezas. 'They need the certainty. Otherwise it eats at them.'

'Has she paid you?'

'On the nose. How about the husband?'

'Not yet.'

'You're running a risk.'

'He won't want his adventures in the papers. Or his wife's.'
'You wouldn't go to the press, would you?'
'No. But I'd like him to think I might.'
'You keep copies of everything?'
'I keep originals. He gets the copies.'

5

Early on Saturday morning, George made a sudden decision to visit Zoe. With the sun still cool as it slanted between the buildings, he collected his car – an old blue Fiat Mirafiori, dented and rust-flecked after years in the war zone of Athens traffic – and drove out along the road to Marathon.

It was a thoughtful journey, between firewood yards, plant nurseries, kitchen and bathroom showrooms, speedboat parks and builders' merchants crammed with brick barbecues – a dreamland of American-style suburban life. Every now and then came a road sign for Marathon, jolting his mind to that ancient battle. Four hundred black ships beached at Schinias. The Persian army, twenty-five thousand strong, camped among the fertile fields, preparing to strike at Athens. And their arrogant general, carting along his own fat block of granite, ready to inscribe it with a memorial of his victory. Nine thousand Greeks – Athenians and Plateans – saw them off. Brilliantly, boldly, driving a wedge of terror through the centre of the enemy lines, scattering their cavalry in panic to flee and drown in the marshes. Their success was improvised, unexpected. In an exceptional gesture they buried their dead with their weapons and horses on the battlefield. And carved the presumptuous granite into a statue of Nemesis.

George liked to visit the site, which was still a chessboard of green fields between the mountains and the sea, with its olive groves and irrigation ditches, a peaceful place where the best of Greece was preserved. A grassy mound held the remains of the Athenian soldiers. One could stand there and be charged with their spirit, still strong after two and a half thousand years. A little museum, built by a patriotic ship-owner, displayed the statues and urns, the bronze tripods and gold jewellery, of a cave sacred to Pan, an ancient cemetery, a Roman temple to Isis.

There were some who compared Greece today to the way it was in 490 B.C., drawing dark parallels between the invading Persians and the International Monetary Fund. As if the Persians had been a team of technocrats and economists, bringing nothing more sinister than administrative reforms and the rule of law! George winced at the idiocy of it. Like every Greek he was fascinated by the past, but he was disgusted when it became an excuse for avoiding the responsibilities of the present.

Thirty kilometres out of town, he turned off for Rafina, and drove slowly down to the port. At the sight of the sea his heart lightened. The next ferry for Andros was leaving in half an hour.

He arrived at the house to find Zoe in the kitchen, wearing an old green apron, the table piled with apricots. She had been busy all morning stripping the trees. She offered him a hot cheek to kiss.

'This is a surprise,' she said.

'I came on impulse. Had a tough week.'

'I'm making jam. Want to help?'

'Sure. Let me have a coffee first.'

He had hoped for a lazy afternoon, but he didn't want an argument.

In fact he enjoyed jam making. The apricots bubbling in

the cauldron, reddening as they cooked, the whole kitchen fragrant. When the syrup thickened, they poured the jam into hot jars, spiking a few 'specials' with raki or brandy, and, fingers scorching, gripping each jar tight in a cloth, they screwed home the lids. It was evening when they finished.

'Let's have a swim,' said Zoe.

They drove down to Aprovato, where the sun hung low over the horizon. George plunged in and swam straight along its track, through flakes of fire. The water was cool and salty, its blue depths darkening as the day dimmed. Zoe followed him, sleek-headed, her face changed by the sea.

He felt young, despite four dozen years on earth. He was still fit, and had managed not to put on weight, unlike many of his friends who sat behind desks all day, never walked further than thirty metres, and lived in a state of gluttonous lethargy. He enjoyed exercise – running, tennis, working out in the park, but most of all swimming, pushing through the water, every muscle engaged, gravity-free, dissolving the toxins of city life.

They drove to Costa's taverna on the hill, drank a bottle of retsina and ate sea bass grilled on charcoal with a sauce of lemon and olive oil. They remembered their early married years, before Nick was born. Life had been easy. Whole summers had gone by between the sea, taverna and bed. Later came the realisations. Nothing happens without effort, children and work take up every moment of the day. Even fruit trees need care.

Zoe had suffered from this awakening. Somehow it led to an affair. A ship-owner, with houses in Switzerland, New York and Paris. Everything done by servants. Even shopping. For twelve months it had thrilled her. Then suddenly she was home again, among the plates and laundry, saying very little.

Was she happy to be back? She never said. But she was back: that was the important thing.

These memories were unspoken, and familiar to them both. They ran parallel to the conversation.

She asked him about Athens. The TV had shown strikes, protests against the government. The Prime Minister, George Papandreou, gave daily speeches, even on foreign visits. He stressed the need for solidarity, for sacrifice. Greece had staved off bankruptcy with a rescue loan, but this came with strict conditions. 'The Greek people,' said Papandreou, 'have no choice but to accept.'

But the Greek people – at least a well-organised minority of them – had no intention of accepting their 'orders from Washington and Brussels'. Let the plutocrats pay! It was their tax-dodging and profiteering that had plunged the country into crisis.

'How bad is it?' she asked.

'Not as bad as it looks. Life goes on as normal.'

'And the protests?'

'They take place in front of parliament. Everywhere else, peace and quiet.'

'What are people saying?'

'Depends who you talk to. People who are comfortably off say it's pay-up time, previous governments borrowed too much, now we must stop spending and put our house in order. We can't do it ourselves, so we need help. On Wednesday I heard a man say he would welcome a German and an IMF official in every public office in Greece. Just to put everything straight. Working people say it's not their fault, so why are they forced to pay? They're resentful. And the communists and anarchists are pouring petrol on the flames.'

She nodded. Then, as if continuing a previous line of thought, 'You remember those three young people who died in a bank a few weeks ago?'

'In May? The fire-bombing?'

'That's right. My cousin Evi's son, Panos, knew one of them. The pregnant girl.'

'That's terrible.'

'In fact it was four who died. Including the unborn baby.'

'You wonder what these idiots were thinking as they threw their molotov cocktails,' said George. 'Some fool of a spokesman was callous enough to say the bank workers deserved to be punished!'

'What for?'

'Ignoring the call for a general strike.'

'That's sick.'

'Those bastards will never be brought to justice. They wore masks, hooded jackets.'

'I wish you'd look into it, George!'

He frowned. 'I can only do that if someone hires me.'

'I could suggest it to the family.'

'Please don't.'

'Why?'

'They'll want special rates.'

'They're not like that.'

'Please – no!'

'You're odd sometimes,' she said.

'I don't work for family.'

'Even if the family's desperate?'

'They should let the police do what they can first.'

'I'm just sad for my nephew, and for the girl's family. I want to do something for them.'

'Of course.'

'Try to help, George!'

'I'll give them some general advice. They can go to one of my colleagues. Pezas is a good man.'

She glared at him.

This was typical of their meetings. The potential was there for old affection to grow again. For a while they seemed to feel it. Then it was gone again. And it seemed too far to reach, too humbling to their pride. As they left the taverna and drove home along the mountain road, they retreated into private thoughts. Back at the house, they changed for bed, took turns to wash, and, he in pyjamas, she in a nightdress, switched on their reading lamps and opened their separate books. They were soon asleep.

In the morning Zoe rose early, made coffee and toast, and labelled the jars: "George & Zoe's Apricot Jam, Andros, June 2010". Symbol of a happy union which did not really exist. A pious hope. Perhaps if they tried hard enough, and often enough, and didn't talk too much about difficult things, the hope might take root and grow.

George came into the kitchen and saw the subliminal message, repeated along the rows of jars. It seemed improbable. Like trying to walk back along the road of time, turning the boiled and sugared fruit back into fresh apricots on the tree. An impossible alchemy.

They had breakfast on the terrace, among the roses and pots of basil. Birds sang in the trees. The valley was ablaze with morning light. The apricots were preserved now, thought George, even if the bloom had gone. Could they hope for anything more?

6

On Monday, back in Athens, George sat in the Café Agamemnon sipping coffee and planning his week. This was his local – a dozen metal tables under the arcades of Aristotle Street. The sun shone brightly among the buildings, casting deep diagonal shadows. Buses and scooters whizzed by, old Captain Andreas wandered through selling lottery tickets, and a canary twittered on a balcony above. Dimitri served his customers with dignity and grace, even though his wife was dying. This part of Athens George loved. It was still a neighbourhood, where experience was shared and the pain of city life eased away by wisecracks, coffee and cigarettes.

George reached for the newspaper on the next table. At once he wished he hadn't. "Suicide of a member of parliament" ran the headline. His pulse quickened as he read. Angelos Boiatzis had left his apartment yesterday afternoon to take his dog for a walk. Two hours later, he had failed to return. His wife went out to look for him. Alerted by their barking dog, she made for a clump of pine trees, where she found her husband on the ground, a pistol in his hand, a blackened hole in his shirt. In a statement to police Mrs Boiatzis said that he had left no note. She was at a loss to explain this tragic event. An article on page three analysed a political career brutally cut short.

George was starting to read this when his phone rang.

'George? It's Hector. Have you heard the news?'

'I was just reading the paper.'

'I wish to God I'd listened to you!'

'About what?'

'Giving the evidence to Mrs Kakridis. She must have had it out with her husband and threatened to expose him. He then hit back with the information you gave him, and threatened to expose Boiatzis. I'm sure that's what drove him to kill himself!'

'Hold on, Hector! That's a hell of a stretch. Do you know any of this for a fact?'

'It's obvious!'

'Nothing's obvious. All I see is a lot of questions.'

'Have you seen the obituaries?'

'I was just reading one.'

'Read them,' said Pezas. 'He was a hero.'

'So?'

'I feel like shit because I failed to protect a decent man. One of the rare ones.'

'You were paid to do a job.'

'I should have listened to you!'

'Listen to me now. Forget all this. It's not your fault.'

A silence greeted this remark.

'Hector?'

'I don't find that a helpful thought,' said Pezas. 'I like to think I'm doing some good.'

'Then stay out of marital work. It's a shitty business.'

'It's ninety percent of my income.'

'Then you're in the wrong game. Go and open a pet shop instead.'

'I may well do that.'

'I'll bet Boiatzis shot himself for some totally unrelated reason.'

'Let's hope so. I tell you I'm feeling bad…'

'Stop it, Hector, save your energy for better things.'

Pezas rang off and George returned to the article. Boiatzis, said the writer, was an idealist who had gone into politics for all the right reasons and only achieved a modest success. "Although widely respected," the piece concluded, "he lacked the aggression that alone achieves results in our cut-throat political culture."

'Amen,' said George.

His phone buzzed again. It was Kakridis, telling him to get over to his office at once. He would not say what it was about.

George finished his coffee and set off on foot for the parliament building.

It was a twenty minute walk, down to Panepistimiou and along to Syntagma Square. There were few signs of crisis on the way: a gipsy beggar or two, some anarchist graffiti. The luxury shops still looked busy, the ladies coming and going with the same expensive hair-dos, the same couture, handbags and jewellery.

For once Kakridis did not keep him waiting.

'This business with Boiatzis,' he said, the moment his office door was closed, 'is a bloody disaster.'

George nodded.

'I'm looking ahead,' said Kakridis. 'To the further damage this can do.'

'In what way?'

'Use your head, man! He was having an affair with my wife!'

'Is that why he killed himself?'

'How the hell should I know? There are so many reasons to shoot yourself these days, he could take his pick!'

'Did you confront your wife about the affair?'

'That's none of your business.'

'Fair enough,' said George. 'So why have you called me in?'

Kakridis scowled, his eyes glinting. 'I don't want anyone making connections between me, my wife and Boiatzis! Police, press, anyone! This story does not exist, understood? Your investigation never took place. I want all photographs and recordings destroyed at once. Your files, correspondence, emails, everything.'

'You don't want an invoice for my work?'

'Are you joking? Nothing!'

'You'll pay me cash?'

'Just let me know the amount.'

'Three thousand.'

'I'll get it to you.'

'OK. As soon as I receive that I'll forget the case.'

'No. You forget it right now. Destroy the evidence!'

'You have nothing to fear at my end. My records are secure. They will be destroyed as soon as I'm paid.'

Kakridis glared at him. 'That's blackmail!'

George returned his gaze calmly. 'Not blackmail. Just standard policy. Which is also a form of insurance.'

'Blackmail! Pure and simple!'

George stood up. Kakridis continued to rant. 'If any of this comes out, I'll know exactly who's to blame.'

'Just pay your bills, Mr Kakridis.'

He turned and left the room, closing the door on some of the filthiest language he had heard in a while.

Out in the street a demonstration had started. A crowd faced dense ranks of riot police in front of the parliament, chanting and shouting. The mood was tense and angry. He read the banners held up above the heads of the crowd. No to austerity! No to orders from Washington! Let the plutocrats pay! We pay our taxes, politicians, how about you?

7

Back at his desk, George thought about how to contact the Chief of Police in Aegina, Captain Bagatzounis. This required tact and leverage. No point ringing up unannounced. Bagatzounis would only speak to senior officers and personal friends – assuming he had any.

He considered the possibilities. One: the British Embassy, in case the professor had become a UK citizen. That was likely to be complicated. He would keep it in reserve. Two: Pazarakis, Chief of the Athens Police. Pazarakis had been helpful in the past, but he was a harassed man, badly organised and prone to panic, with a daily avalanche of work and too few staff. Crimes were not so much solved as buried in paperwork.

There was only one person left: Takis Mitropoulos, his friend in the Kalamata police, down in the southern Peloponnese. George owed him more favours than he cared to remember, but Takis seemed not to count them.

He dialled.

'George! I'm driving. What do you want?'

'A way in to the Aegina police.'

'What for?'

'I'm on a case there. I need to find out what they know. The man there is a certain Bagatzounis.'

'Bagatzounis? What kind of a name is that? Sounds like a pimp.'

'I don't care about his family history, I just need to talk to him.'

'I'll work on it.'

Next he rang Madame Corneille's friend Abbas, who had been at dinner with the professor the night before he died. Abbas was Persian but sounded entirely American. When George asked him who he thought might have shot the professor, Abbas said, 'There's a whole coop full of candidates. You've got your work cut out.' Invited to elaborate, he said, 'You'll have to come over to the island and get to know the scene.'

'That sounds time-consuming.'

'Shortcuts will lead to the wrong places.'

'I was hoping you might guide me.'

'I can try.'

'Do you know a retired colonel who lives in the house behind Madame Corneille?'

'Colonel Varzalis?'

'That's the one.'

'He's an old friend.'

'Do you think he might have done it?'

'I doubt it. Unless he was shooting pigeons and hit the professor by accident.'

'Is that possible?'

'Anything's possible, but Varzalis was an Olympic marksman. He doesn't miss much.'

'You don't think he would have shot him deliberately?'

'No way.'

'You know him well?'

'We go back a long way.'

'How come?'

'We met at the Athens Rifle Club, about twenty years ago.'

George had never heard of the Athens Rifle Club. Abbas

gave him the history – founded by British officers after the First World War, kept going by a bunch of local and expatriate eccentrics.

'Are you still a member?'

'I am. But haven't pulled a trigger for nearly a decade. Certainly not on March 25th this year, in case you're wondering.'

'I wasn't.'

'Come and see me next time you're over.'

George said he would. The voice echoed in his mind. Sharp, clever, ironic. A friend of the colonel's. Both of them gun enthusiasts. That would need looking into.

He was on the way to the bathroom when Taki called.

'I've asked around about your police chief in Aegina. He's a prick apparently, and he'll give you trouble if he can. Your best bet is a man called Sotiriou, at Violent Crimes. He's senior to Bagatzounis, stratospherically senior, and this case is under his jurisdiction.'

'Can I have his number?'

'No.'

'He won't talk to me?'

'No.'

'Another prick?'

'You could say that.'

'This is going to be fun.'

'I've spoken to him. He'll talk to Bagatzounis.'

'That's better than nothing.'

'This is a sticky case. Everyone's very cautious. You can ring Bagatzounis any time.'

George's ear was aching from the telephone. He busied himself with tidying and filing. He locked away the folder of papers on Kakridis, just to be safe. Then he fixed himself a cup of coffee and rang the police station in Aegina.

'Yes? Speak!'

'I'm looking for Captain Bagatzounis.'

'You've got him! Who are you?'

'George Zafiris, private investigator.'

'What do you want?'

'I'm researching the Petrakis murder.'

'On whose authority?'

'I'm working for Constantine Petrakis, brother of –'

'I know the individual. He has already been to see me. I've told him everything there is to know.'

'I come on the recommendation of Colonel Sotiriou of the Violent Crimes Unit.'

The voice changed at once, losing its arrogance. 'Colonel Sotiriou?'

'I believe he has phoned you.'

There was a silence at the other end of the line. George waited.

'Hello, Mr Zafiris?'

'Yes?'

'Can you come here at eight tomorrow morning?'

'Where?'

'Police station, Aegina.'

'I'll be there.'

He's a prick all right, thought George.

At six that evening, he stepped off the Aegina ferry, an overnight bag on his shoulder. He walked the length of the waterfront, picking a careful route between the café tables. From one of these came a greeting: 'Mr Zafiris!'

He looked round, and saw Madame Corneille sitting with a white-haired man of aquiline looks. They were drinking ouzo.

Madame Corneille introduced him.

'Jalal Abbas. How do you do?'

They shook hands. George noticed his precise features, a smooth, coppery skin, sharp blue eyes.

'Will you join us for a drink?'

'In half an hour? I need to check into my hotel.'

'We'll be here.'

George walked to the Hotel Brown. He took his key and climbed the stairs, threw open the window in his room and lay down on the bed, listening lazily to the wheels of horse-drawn calèches rattling along the harbour front. On the ceiling, reflections of sea light trembled as shadows passed across them. He closed his eyes.

It was a micro-sleep, but it did him good. He rose, took a shower, and quickly dressed. Pen, notebook, phone, money… he was ready.

Madame Corneille was no longer there when he reached the café. Abbas apologised on her behalf, saying she had an appointment with a client. George waved it aside.

'So,' said Abbas, 'four hours ago I invite you to Aegina, and now, as if by royal command, here you are.'

'I've come to meet the local police chief.'

'Aha!' Abbas's eyes sparkled maliciously. 'Why would a man do that?'

'To move my inquiries forward.'

'That's a tactical error.'

'Maybe,' said George, 'but he told me to come.'

'Bagatzounis will move your enquiries backwards!'

'Really?'

Abbas nodded. 'That's his style. He will drain you of everything: understanding, hope, belief in humanity…' He flung a handful of cocktail nuts into his mouth and crunched vigorously. 'Talk to anyone but him.'

'I'll try to keep myself undrained,' said George.

'You'll have to or you're finished. Who else do you plan to meet?'

'Colonel Varzalis. If that's possible.'

'It's possible. Want me to call him?'

'Sure.'

'You're aware that he suffers from Alzheimer's?'

'No.'

'It's important.'

'Of course.'

Abbas drew a phone from his pocket, dialled, and spoke briefly in Greek.

'Eight thirty,' he said. 'That gives us an hour. What else can I help you with?'

'You said I should get to know the scene.'

'Damn right!'

'Well? Where do I begin?'

'You begin with a drink. Ouzo? Whisky?'

'Ouzo.'

Abbas snapped his fingers and placed the order. He leaned back in his chair. 'You're looking for a killer. So let's forget about all the normal people, shall we? We look at the weirdos. I know them all. I've studied them. Every island has its share, both local and imported. The foreigners are usually *artistes* of some description, many of them rather unfocussed personalities suffering from the delusion that wearing dark glasses and drinking in cafés all day is going to turn them into James Joyce. I assume you know the type.'

'Not personally.'

'You're lucky. They range from the harmlessly feeble-minded to menacing psychopaths. One of these could possibly be the killer. Main objection: they are not generally very effective human beings. The idea that they might be organised enough to find a weapon, ammunition, a spot to shoot from, and a moment of sufficient lucidity and steadiness of hand to hold a rifle straight, especially at seven thirty in the evening, is, frankly, far-fetched. One or two, given the right motivation, enough concentrated hatred, might be capable of it. I can name them. But I know no reason why they would wish to kill Professor Petrakis…'

'How about locals?'

'Several candidates: anarchists, fascists, the disturbed, the angry, the unloved. A few of these have military fantasies, and go round in camouflage trousers to prove it. Given the right motivation, some grudge or insult, or even a paranoid-schizophrenic scenario, one of them might just do it. But what on earth did John Petrakis ever do to offend them?' Abbas grimaced. 'That will take a lot of digging in extremely dark and malodorous places.'

George was curious about the resident foreigners. He asked how many there were.

About a hundred, Abbas thought.

'What brings them here?'

'Oh, every fantasy under the sun. "I lived here in a former existence" – that's a standard one. Or the lure of antiquity. Or nature. The pagan gods. The Orthodox Church. The sea. The light. The mountains. The people. Any damn thing! But the biggest and best is the Byronic impulse to escape failure at home and live in a sunlit land posing as a genius.'

'I trust you don't include yourself in that category?'

'I do not!' said Abbas indignantly. 'I had a job!'

'Which of them could have killed the professor?'

Instead of replying, Abbas sipped his ouzo, his pale blue eyes on the masts of the fishing boats at the quayside.

'There are just two. One is so crazy he wouldn't even need a motive. The other is an evil man whom I know all too well. But I wouldn't want to point the finger at him.'

'Why not?'

'Because he's done me wrong – great wrong! He's an enemy. *The* enemy, to be precise. I suspect him of every crime that's committed on the island… I don't want my vendetta to get in the way of your investigation, so let's forget about him.'

'Could he have killed the professor?'

'I doubt it.'

'What's his name?'

'Ernest Hemingway.'

'You're joking.'

'It's a false name. He thinks it'll make publishers take notice.'

'I'm sure he's right.'

'It's no damn good if you write crap.'

'Who's the other crazy foreigner?'

'Mad Terry. You only meet him by chance. No point looking for him. He moves according to his own celestial timetable… But we must go and find the colonel now. He doesn't like you to be late.'

8

They walked along the harbour front, past Kapodistria and his sad little arc of palm trees, with the great grey rampart of the Peloponnese across the straits to the east. They turned inland, up a long, narrow lane. After two hundred metres the lane opened into a small, well-kept square. To the right a pair of wrought-iron gates were set into a high stone wall. Abbas tugged on the bell-pull. A goat bell clattered above their heads and an old lady in a faded floral dress came hobbling along the garden path.

Abbas kissed her on both cheeks, calling her 'Kyra Sophia'. She led them around the side of the house, past ranks of lemon and orange trees, their trunks white with lime-wash. Behind the house, in a vine-shaded courtyard, a lean old man with close-cut white hair and a precise little moustache sat studying a newspaper under a magnifying glass. At the sound of their steps he looked up, caught sight of Abbas and rose shakily to his feet.

'The Gurkhas have arrived!'

'I'm not a Gurkha, Colonel, as I've often told you. I'm a Parsee.'

'To me you're a Gurkha. You'd better accept it.'

Abbas introduced George.

'Have we met before?' asked the colonel.

'No.'

'Forgive my asking. My memory…'

'No problem,' said George.

The colonel invited them to sit down, indicating the rusting metal chairs around the table. Kyra Sophia asked them what they would like to drink and shuffled away to the kitchen. They discussed the recent hot weather. The colonel seemed absent from the conversation.

'Did you say we've met before?' he asked suddenly.

'No,' said George. 'Not as far as I know.'

The colonel tapped his forehead. 'Empty as an old shoe box.'

'At least you know it,' said Abbas.

'Too well,' said the colonel. Then, to George, 'What are you doing in Aegina?'

'I'm investigating the murder of Professor Petrakis.'

The colonel looked blank. 'Do I know him?'

'That's what I wanted to ask you.'

'I can't remember. What do you think, Abbas?'

'You never mentioned his name to me.'

'There you are then.'

'You knew his brother Constantine.'

'Constantine is a familiar name. Constantine Petrakis. That's a name I would happily forget!'

'Really?'

The colonel scowled. 'We had a disagreement. He behaved badly. He and his even more unpleasant partner. Men from good families, mind you. Proof of the decline of our nation, if proof were needed.'

'What did you disagree about?'

'Have a guess!'

'Money?'

'Correct!'

'What happened?'

'They wanted to build a hotel. Just there.' The colonel pointed to the end of his garden. 'An extremely large and ugly hotel. Unsuitable in every way for a historic town.'

'What happened?'

'I stopped them.'

'How did you do that?'

'With all the means at my disposal.' He took evident satisfaction from the memory.

George was struck by the exactness of the colonel's recollection of this incident. It contrasted oddly with his earlier vagueness.

'I hear from Abbas that you're a great sportsman?'

The colonel nodded. 'Four Olympic Games. Four gold medals.'

'You must have a fine collection of trophies.'

'I do.'

'Do you still shoot?'

'No.'

'You have your guns still?'

'Of course. All in working order.'

'But you don't use them?'

The colonel's eyes narrowed. 'Only in an emergency.'

'Such as?'

'You never know when your country may need you.'

'One man and a few rifles can't do much.'

'No, but a group of armed men, skilled in the arts of war, can cause endless trouble to an invader. History provides many examples.'

'You're prepared for an invasion?'

'I am.'

'By the International Monetary Fund perhaps?'

The colonel seem not to understand the reference. 'By

anyone at all,' he said.

'Can you call on a group of volunteers?'

'I can!'

Intrigued, George said, 'I would be curious to see your arsenal.'

The colonel stood up smartly. 'Come on, Abbas, let's show him. He won't rest easy until we do.'

The colonel led the way across the yard to the back door, where they met Kyra Sophia on her way out with a tray of drinks.

'We're going to the library,' said the colonel. 'Bring the drinks up there please.'

'Certainly, Colonel.'

They entered a hall paved with chessboard squares of polished marble. A Murano chandelier threw dappled light on a pair of oil portraits from the 1920s: a pin-stripe-suited entrepreneur smiling prosperously from his desk with a cigar in one hand, and a hollow-eyed beauty in pale silk with a gardenia in her hair.

'My wife's family,' said the colonel.

They climbed a marble staircase, passing a series of coloured engravings of Egypt.

At the head of the stairs the colonel led them through a heavy double door into a room with tall windows shuttered against the summer light. He switched on a lamp. Bookshelves with glazed doors lined the walls. To the right, one bay of shelves was replaced by a gun rack.

The colonel moved towards a table in the centre of the room, where a glass display case held an array of medals, sporting and military, the four Olympic golds in a prominent position. The atmosphere was hushed, opulent. A gentleman's club-room, transplanted from London.

George strolled along the shelves, noting the colonel's interests: military history, archaeology, art, antiques. He came to the gun rack.

'These look like collector's items,' he said.

'Correct,' said the colonel. He produced a small bunch of keys on a silver chain. 'Let's take a look.'

The doors swung open. With swift hands the colonel lifted a shotgun from the rack. He broke it open, checked the barrels, snapped it shut and handed it to George. 'Put that to your shoulder.'

George tried it, aiming the gun at a corner of the ceiling. He was amazed by its lightness, the way it flew to the shoulder, resting comfortably in his hands.

'That's not a gun, it's a violin,' he said, handing it back.

'It's all in the balance,' said the colonel. 'This shotgun weighs just under three kilograms. If the weight were not so beautifully distributed it would feel like thirty.'

He slotted it back in the rack, moved along a few, and took down a military rifle.

'Try this.'

George shouldered it with difficulty. It was all hard edges and lumpy weight. The wood of the butt felt like granite.

'What is it?'

'Pattern 1914 Enfield. Made in the US by Remington under contract, used by Greek forces in the Albanian campaign of 1940–41. This rifle sent the Italians weeping back to their mothers that winter. It was still in use when I joined up in 1953. I did all my training with it. A rough old weapon, but a trusted friend!'

'That first one, the shotgun, what was that?'

'A Purdey.'

'Any good for shooting?'

'Oh yes. A lovely thing all round.'

'What about your Olympic shooting? What did you use for that?'

The colonel lifted another rifle from the rack. Slim, smooth, snake-like in its elegance. George raised it to his shoulder. It was even lighter than the Purdey, the barrel a thin dark shaft ending in a tiny fin.

'What's this one?'

'A Hämmerli.'

'Can you still use it?'

'Of course.'

'I'd love to see you shoot something.'

'Not in here!'

'We could open the windows?'

'All right. Would you mind, Abbas?'

As Abbas unfastened the windows, Kyra Sophia appeared with the tray of drinks.

'Thank you,' said the colonel. 'There on the table, please.'

'Can I bring anything else for you?'

'No thank you.'

'You shouldn't shoot any more, sir.'

'I know, Sophia, thank you. It's quite safe.'

'Watch what he does, Mr Abbas,' she said. 'I don't like it.' She left the room, pulling the double doors after her.

Abbas swung the shutters open to a sky full of swallows, wheeling and twittering in the fading light. George rested his hands on the windowsill. About thirty metres away stood the two-storey house with Madame Corneille's bathroom window clearly visible. George glanced at the colonel. The old man was looking up at the sky, which had turned scarlet in the evening sun, alive and swirling with wings.

'Could you hit a swallow?' asked George.

'I would never wish to.'

'How about a seagull?' He pointed to a trio of seabirds patrolling above the rooftops.

'They would be an easy target,' said the colonel, 'but why take a life?'

George pointed to a small patch of discoloured plaster on the wall beside the bathroom window.

'There's a target. Try that.'

The colonel turned his steely eyes on him.

'Only a delinquent would shoot at a point so near a window.'

'Why?'

'Suppose I miss?'

'I don't expect you to miss.'

'I shan't, but still! Safety first!'

'Look up there,' said Abbas. 'There's a child's balloon, making a break for freedom.'

George watched the coloured speck rising slowly above the roofs of the upper town. He heard the mechanical click of the rifle opening, a rattle of ammunition in a tin. The colonel stepped forward, alert as a cocker spaniel, the rifle held lightly in his hands. There was a sharp crack and the balloon vanished.

The colonel stood still for a moment, as if he planned a second shot. Then, with a nod, brought the rifle down from his shoulder.

'That must have been a good 300 metres,' said Abbas.

'I'm still capable,' said the colonel.

George thanked him for the demonstration. The colonel passed the Hämmerli to Abbas and asked him to hang it in the gun rack.

'It's strange,' said George, 'but Professor Petrakis was shot from a position very similar to this.'

'Who's that?' said the colonel.

'John Petrakis. We were talking about him earlier.'

'I knew another Petrakis.'

'Constantine. His brother.'

'That's right! Why do you mention him?'

'He was shot. Through that window, right there!'

'I told you, guns are dangerous things!'

'He would have been clearly visible. Framed in that window. A very tempting target.'

The colonel pulled a face. 'You have some strange ideas!'

George continued to press him. 'This professor was a controversial figure. He published books on what he called the dark side of ancient Greece.'

'What dark side?'

'Crime, slavery, sex with teenagers, child sacrifice…'

'Oh, that old stuff!'

'He was widely respected. Taught at Princeton, London…'

'Mad! Totally mad! Everyone wants to hear about the vices of the giants who built our civilisation. Instead of studying their achievements, learning from them. It's the triumph of small-mindedness!'

'What is curious, Colonel, is that this man was shot on March 25th.'

'So?'

'It suggests a motive.'

The colonel seemed puzzled.

'For a patriot, the professor's books can be seen as an insult to Greece.'

The colonel looked unimpressed. 'It would have to be a patriot of somewhat defective intellect!'

'Why do you say that?'

'Ancient and modern. Separate things.'

'Maybe in your mind, Colonel, but not in others! And

maybe in yours, even, the power of emotion, of anger at this cheapening of the nation's past, the concentration on homosexuality, prostitution, drunken orgies...'

The colonel placed a hand on George's arm. 'I can see this offends you,' he said. 'It offends every Greek. But it's not important. Like a shower of rain on the marble of our temples! A shadow from a passing cloud! Let the pedants of Princeton have their say. Those temples will be admired and studied long after their books have crumbled to dust!'

'Someone was offended enough by those books to shoot the author in the head. Someone standing in a window like this one, with a gun like this. Someone who knew how to shoot!'

The colonel shook his head sadly. 'What a terrible story! Was he a friend of yours?'

'I feel as if he was. I'm investigating his death.'

Varzalis nodded sympathetically.

George pressed him. 'I need samples of your ammunition, Colonel.'

'What for?'

'To compare them with the bullet that killed the professor.'

'Of course. But look here, I don't want you loading them in any guns!'

'I promise.'

'Then take whatever you need.'

Abbas helped provide a sample of ammunition from each of the colonel's six rifles. Six heavy little brass cylinders, tipped with a rounded cone of lead. George held them in the palm of his right hand, let them roll and knock together. Six capsules of death. He slipped them into his trouser pocket.

The three men stood in silence by the open window.

'The drinks!' said Abbas suddenly.

'Ah, of course. Please, gentlemen... Your good health!'

He turned to George. 'Tell me, sir, what is your business in Aegina?'

9

The police station of Aegina occupied two low, poor buildings in an unpaved courtyard. Motorbikes, jeeps and squad cars were parked at odd angles among lemon trees. A concrete path, weed-cracked and littered with cigarette ends, led to a pair of shadowy doorways, one marked "Tourist Police", the other "Officers Room". The signs were painted by a wavering amateur hand in the national colours, blue and white. From the roofs of the buildings a jumble of antennae sprouted like cacti.

George chose the Officers Room. A desk sergeant sat staring at a computer screen while a slender column of cigarette smoke floated up from an ashtray at his elbow. A telephone jangled, unanswered, in a back room.

'I've come to see Captain Bagatzounis,' said George.

'Name?' said the sergeant, eyes still on the screen.

'Zafiris. My appointment is for eight o'clock.'

The sergeant glanced at a clock on the wall and wearily picked up the telephone. He raised the half-finished cigarette to his lips and muttered a few words. The reply seemed excessively long. He stubbed out his cigarette, nodding and saying mechanically, 'Yes, sir. We've done that. Has he not replied yet? Yes, it's in hand… No not yet… We're still waiting…' The sergeant lit another cigarette, nodded, spun the packet to the left, then to the right.. He inhaled and exhaled, listening half-heartedly, returning bland replies. Not once did he make a note, or display a flicker of energy. He sat in his cloud of smoke, frowning, stifling yawns. Having reached the end of the cigarette, he squashed it into the ashtray, and stared at the ceiling while he listened to more instructions. At last he put the telephone down.

'Door on the left,' he said.

George knocked and received a brisk 'Come in!'

Captain Bagatzounis sat behind a rampart of papers at a tiny desk. His face was round and boyish, with plump, pale cheeks, thinning brown hair and a florid moustache. His eyes were persecuted and melancholy. George knew at once it would be a difficult interview.

'I'm here on the recommendation of Colonel Sotiriou,' he said by way of reminder.

Bagatzounis puckered his lips and moved a pile of papers a few centimetres to his left.

'I remember,' he said. 'How is Colonel Sotiriou?'

'He's well. He told me you would be willing to help.'

'Of course.' There was anything but willingness in the voice.

'I've been retained by Mr Constantine Petrakis.'

A frown immediately pinched the smooth brow.

'You know who I mean?' asked George.

'I know only too well!'

'He's lost a brother, so one can understand that he wants results.'

Bagatzounis interrupted him. 'Of course. It's natural. But let me tell you right away, he goes too far. He wants instant results. That's his problem. If only he would let the authorities deal with these matters in the correct way we would all be able to get on with our work more effectively!'

'I have a certain sympathy with that view,' said George, 'but I also have a job to do.'

'Mr Petrakis with his endless questions prevents me doing mine!'

'How is the investigation going, Captain?'

'I'm sorry?'

'Have you had the forensic results?'

Bagatzounis stared at him gravely. 'These are police matters.'

'Can you at least give me a general idea?'

'We're not in charge of this investigation.'

'Who is?'

'GADA.'

'What's your role?'

'Local knowledge and support.'

'Do you have a register of local gun owners?'

'Of course.'

'Can I see it?'

'No.'

'Why not?'

'It's not a public document.'

'I'm not the public.'

'The rules are the rules.'

'And this is Greece.'

Bagatzounis stiffened. 'Where the laws of civilisation were first written!'

'That may be true,' said George, 'but it hasn't stopped us breaking them on a daily basis ever since.'

'Our nation needs respect for the law, Mr Zafiris!'

'There's a difference between the spirit and the letter.'

Bagatzounis raised a hand, as if he were stopping traffic. 'Distinctions of that kind are the domain of judges and priests. They're too subtle for me. My job is to uphold the law exactly as it is written.'

George felt his frustration rising. He switched the line of argument.

'Have you seen the forensic report?'

'No.'

'Have you provided a list of possible suspects?'

'To whom?'

'GADA, the DAEEB, or anyone else?'

Bagatzounis hesitated before replying: 'I have had several conversations with the investigating authorities.'

'Can you tell me anything about the leads they might be following, or anyone you think might be involved?'

'All that is strictly confidential.'

'Of course,' said George. 'But with respect, Captain, you're taking this the wrong way.'

'I'll take it any way I want!'

'I can help you.'

'How?'

'You have all my knowledge at your disposal.'

Bagatzounis drew himself up to his full unimpressive height. 'Are you telling me that you have information material to this investigation?'

'Let me pursue my inquiries,' said George, 'give me some help, and there's a good chance I'll get a result.'

Bagatzounis seemed annoyed. 'Either you have information or you don't!'

'At this stage I do have some information. Some, I repeat. Not enough. But I need your co-operation.'

'I can take a statement any time.'

'That's not what I'm offering.'

'Then I suggest you continue your investigation until you can offer it.'

'There's no point in my duplicating your work!'

'That's not my problem.'

'Isn't the murder your problem? Doesn't it look bad on your record? Doesn't it look bad for Aegina?'

'I've told you, we're not handling the case.'

'OK! It's Athens. But the murder happened here! How about getting hold of a progress report?'

Bagatzounis was uninterested.

'Why not telephone GADA and ask?' said George.

'I can do whatever I think fit. But they are not accountable to me, and I am certainly not accountable to you!'

'I'm just asking for co-operation.'

'I know exactly what you're asking for! A short cut. But there are no short cuts. Not through this office!'

George took a deep breath.

'I'd like you to consider my proposition,' he said. 'If you think I can help you, or you can help me, give me a call.'

He placed his business card on the policeman's desk. Bagatzounis ignored it.

'One more thing,' said George. 'I need a list of residents in the area to the south of Aghios Nektarios Street.'

'What for?'

'I want to check them for gun licences.'

'The list of residents won't tell you that.'

'I know. But if I can compare the two lists, residents and gun owners, I'll have some names to work on. If I had the forensic report I could narrow the list down, possibly even pinpoint the killer.'

Bagatzounis nodded wearily. 'That is what we're all trying to do.'

'Do you think they've done that in Athens?'

'I can't tell you.'

'Why not?'

'I'm not prepared to say any more.'

'May I see the list of residents?'

'No.'

'Don't tell me that's confidential!'

'It is.'

'But why? I could just walk round and read the names off the doorbells.'

'I suggest you do that.'

'I'm trying to save time.'

'By taking up mine!'

George stood up. 'This is ridiculous. I shall tell Colonel Sotiriou that you've obstructed me in every possible way.'

Bagatzounis sighed self-righteously. 'I'm sure the colonel understands the situation a great deal better than you do.'

10

Raw with anger, George walked quickly along the waterfront. He wanted to drive his fists into something, smash it to bits. Bagatzounis was an imbecile. Obstructive, pompous, narrow-minded. He presumed to lecture others on Greek civilisation! The stupidity of the man seemed, in George's mind, to infect the whole of his nation – a nation of compulsive law-breakers. The laws were ever more elaborate in their complexity, the people ever more ingenious in their evasions. Each tormented the other. A ludicrous chain of official documents had become necessary to carry out the simplest transactions: buy a car, sell a house, open a shop. Ministries to visit, stamps and signatures to obtain from self-important officials who rarely bothered to show up for work, resented it on the few days when they did, and often demanded bribes to do anything at all. In the midst of this swamp of hatred, laziness and corruption sat these misguided and ridiculous upholders of the law, who blocked up the whole system with their sermons and delusions…

He reached a kiosk and bought a bottle of water. He drank it in the church garden, contemplating Kapodistria's marble brow, wondering what the great man would have made of the monstrous system of government he had given birth to; whether, in the light of history, he might not feel grateful to have been shot dead by an angry warlord as he came out of church one October morning.

He drained the bottle, dropped it in a bin, and set off up the first of the lanes that led away from the shore. At Afeas Street he turned right, parallel to the coast, among butchers, grocers and ironmongers – useful shops, not the traders in luxury trivia, the nail salons and pet-product suppliers that clogged the streets of Athens. The weather was bright, the shadows deep and cool. At a fork in the road he came to the school, where children were shouting and hurling themselves around a basketball court shaded by a line of eucalyptus trees. He followed the trees towards the sea, letting his footsteps lead him.

He found himself in front of a bookshop. In the window, displayed among sentimental novels and books about astrology, money and alternative health, he spotted *The Darkness of Ancient Greece* by John Petrakis.

He asked to see a copy. It was a Greek translation, published last year. The photograph of the author showed a man in his fifties with a clear-eyed, ironic gaze; a man amused by life.

'Have you sold many copies?' he asked.

'Around thirty,' said the bookseller, a thin, pale, earnest man.

'Since the murder or before?'

'Mainly since.'

'Is thirty a lot?'

'For a serious book, it is.'

'I've heard it's shocking.'

'I wouldn't describe it as shocking.'

'How would you describe it?'

'Direct and powerful.'

'You've read it?'

'Of course.'

'And recommend it?'

'Totally.'

'Why?'

'It's exceptionally well written, by an expert in the field. He says things we need to hear.'

'Trashing the ancient Greeks?'

'That's not what he does. He acknowledges their genius, and their imperfections. He sees them accurately, as human beings. Not as heroes.'

'We need heroes. Desperately.'

'We do. Believable ones. Then, perhaps,' the bookseller fixed him with melancholy eyes, 'we can stop despising ourselves as a nation.'

'If the book does all that,' said George, 'I'll have it.'

He began to walk towards the port. There were only a few more things he could do in Aegina that day. Try the town hall for a register of residents. Maybe talk to Madame Corneille. Then head back to Athens.

He was not ready for another bureaucratic mauling, but decided to get it over with. The worst they could do was say no. By expecting the worst he could not be disappointed. But the clerk at the town hall surprised him. She handed him the register without hesitation.

His mood lifted by this gift of fate, George looked up the names of the property owners. Owners were not necessarily the same as residents, of course, but he had a sense at last of making progress, of existing in a rational world. There was no point taking down names now. Better to check the firearms register first – if he was ever allowed to see it.

He thanked the clerk and walked the short distance to Madame Corneille's.

She came to the door in bare feet, jeans and white shirt, a necklace of amber beads around her neck. Her face lit up at the sight of him, although her eyes quickly shadowed with concern.

'You don't have the aura you had the other day,' she said.

'I'm not surprised.'

'What's happened?'

'Nothing. Literally nothing. That's the problem.'

'Come in and have some coffee.'

They sat in her kitchen among crystals and sacred images from Tibet. A different incense was burning today, rose-scented. She served Greek coffee flavoured with cardamom, in the Arab style.

'So,' he said, trying hard not to sound sceptical, 'you can actually see the aura around a person, can you?'

'I can.'

'What does it look like?'

'A coloured oval around the head and body.'

'What is it? A mood indicator?'

'It's much more than that! It's an energy field that reveals the entire condition of the mind, body and soul.'

'Can you give me an example?'

'I've just seen yours. It shows a mind in a restless, troubled state.'

'How do you know that's not just body language?'

'Body language is significant, of course. But it's ambiguous. You can slouch because of tiredness or a bad back, yet your spirit may be relatively strong. The aura is an X-ray of the soul.'

'One colour or many?'

'Rainbow-coloured.'

'Can anyone see it?'

'If they open their eyes, they can. But many of us have forgotten how to see it, or been conditioned out of it.'

'And when you've seen it, what do you do?'

'You can use it for therapy, for balancing, or just a friendly conversation.'

'I noticed you spoke to Constantine Petrakis about his aura the first time I came here.'

'Did I?'

She let him understand with a glance that this was not a subject to pursue. He decided to go on just the same.

'I was hoping to ask you about him and Colonel Varzalis.'

'What about them? '

'There seems to have been a clash.'

Again the reluctance, a hesitation. Then quietly: 'There was.'

'Over what?'

'A hotel.'

'Can you tell me any more?'

'I don't know any more.'

'How well do you know the colonel?'

'Hardly at all. He's not my type.'

'I'm a little surprised that you find Constantine Petrakis your type.'

'Did I say I find him my type?'

'Perhaps not… And John? He was your type?'

'Absolutely! You could only love him.'

'Did you?'

'Did I what? Love him?'

George said nothing. She knew what he meant.

'I loved him as a friend,' she said. 'There was no question of anything else.'

He asked what had brought her to Aegina. She told him she had been a dancer in her youth, first in the French National Ballet, then at the Folies Bergères – 'a necessary change of rhythm', she said, 'as well as of costume'. Later she joined a contemporary dance company in Bordeaux. After ten years of that she became interested in photography. Then, after two children, a difficult divorce and 'a spiritual crisis in which I discovered my true powers', she became a therapist and spiritual adviser.

'Is that your job now?'

'If you can call it a job.'

'What do you call it?'

'I call it a practice.'

'Is Constantine one of your clients?'

She said nothing.

'I see. I'm not supposed to ask.'

'You can ask,' she said, 'but you won't always get an answer.'

He finished his coffee. 'I should get moving,' he said.

'You haven't told me your story.'

'You want to hear it?'

'Naturally.'

'It's simple. I grew up in Athens, studied in London, worked as an economist at the National Bank. Ten years of office life, high-powered talk, fiscal theory. I earned good money, but it wasn't for me. I lived in a one-dimensional universe of numbers, and I felt I was suffocating. So I took a job with an investigation agency.'

'In England?'

'No, Athens. With a man called Karakitsis – you may have heard of him.'

She shook her head.

'He was the prince of investigators. Perfect mixture of rogue and gentleman. Switched from one to the other in a moment. In fact, he was both at the same time.'

'Did you find what you were looking for?'

'What do you mean?'

'In changing your profession. Did you escape the one-dimensional universe of numbers?'

'I suppose so.'

'Are you satisfied?'

'When I reach the end of an investigation I'm satisfied. Until then I'm – how did you put it? – restless and troubled.'

'It may be that you are engaged in a deeper spiritual search which no amount of criminal investigation will satisfy.'

'You may very well be right.'

'I sense it strongly.'

George bristled. This was getting bullshitty. 'You could say that about every single human being on earth.'

'Does that make it any less true?'

'No. Just a bit less my particular problem.'

He finished his coffee. 'I must get back to the city,' he said.

'Each of us needs to solve the problem in our own way,' she said.

'Agreed.' George stood up. 'Thanks for the coffee.'

11

Colonel Sotiriou's office, in a back street behind Leoforos Alexandras, was a nightmare version of all the other police offices he had known in Greece. Grim metal furniture, walls unpainted for decades, grubby old computers trussed in their cables, a desk heaped like a builder's yard with files. These were the standard features, but in this place the paperwork had multiplied insanely, with stacks knee-high all over the floor. The walls were lined with bookshelves, every inch crammed with ring binders, boxes, folders and bundles of documents tied with ribbon. The air smelt of dust and stale tobacco smoke. The light from the courtyard window, filtered through dirty panes, was yellow-brown.

The colonel was a gaunt man with a weary face, short, bald, grey-skinned. He crushed a cigarette into an ashtray as George came in. There was a single chair – tubular chrome, cracked green leatherette cushions. He was invited to sit down, finding room for his feet wherever he could among the documents.

Sotiriou asked after Takis Mitropoulos. George said he had seen him last month in Kalamata.

'He's a hard worker,' said Sotiriou. 'But he has his struggles.'

'Because he's honest.'

'Maybe.' Sotiriou smirked bitterly. 'It's no fun being a policeman any more. When I joined the force thirty years ago, there was no violent crime. Nothing to speak of. A few family quarrels, honour killings in the villages – remember them? Seems like the Stone Age now! But we had things under control. Today it's war. A torrent of crime! Vicious stuff – against immigrants, by immigrants, the poor getting pushed ever more to the margins. We don't have time to solve a quarter of what's thrown at us.'

'So what's changed?'

'Greed, consumer values, a decline in religion and family, immigrants from desperate countries…'

'Such as?'

'Oh, plenty to choose from! First it was Albania, then Pakistan, Georgia, Russia… These are people who kill for a few euros. They've taught us their ways. Instead of us civilising them, we let them barbarise us.' He reached for a fresh cigarette. 'How can I help you?'

'A murder in Aegina.'

'Which one?'

'Professor Petrakis.'

Sotiriou nodded. 'Rifle shot through the head, March 25th. Very bizarre. What have you found?'

'Nothing much. I've been obstructed by the local police. I want to get back to the main story, the main evidence.'

'Which is what, as you see it?'

'There are about twenty houses the shot could have been fired from. With the firearms register for Aegina you could narrow down the list of suspects to a handful of people. With the forensic report as well you'd find the killer.'

'Only twenty houses, you say?'

'At most.'

'You've been there, had a look?'

'Of course.'

'Who's paying you?'

'The brother of the deceased.'

'Name?'

'Constantine Petrakis.'

Sotiriou did not react to the name.

'Has he told you why he's hired a private investigator?'

'He says the police are doing nothing.'

'Is that your impression too?'

'I don't know. The local chief, Bagatzounis, told me they're overworked. Yet his duty sergeant sits at his desk playing poker on the internet.'

Sotiriou frowned. 'That's bad management. But standard for the provinces. What do you propose?'

'I would be happy just to see those two documents. Firearms register and forensic report.'

'And then what?'

'Then it may well be possible to make an arrest.'

'Perfect.'

'Can you help?'

Sotiriou shrugged his shoulders. 'I can try. There is a problem, however.'

'What's that?'

'We don't have sergeants playing poker in this building. We are genuinely overworked. Every office looks like this one, jammed with ongoing investigations. These are dealt with in strict chronological order.'

George attempted to make light of it. 'Surely nothing is done chronologically in Greece!'

'In this office it is.'

George said nothing. He gave Sotiriou a sceptical look.

'You're hoping to jump the queue,' said Sotiriou.

'If there was a queue,' said George, 'I would happily stand in it all day.'

'In here, Mr Zafiris, there is a queue. No one jumps it. Minister, film star, ship-owner, they all wait their turn.'

'I don't believe it,' said George

'Just watch!'

'I don't have time.'

'Then you must find it, because time is what this is going to take.'

'If it's a question of money, a donation to the Police Benevolent Fund….'

'It won't help. In fact it's a criminal suggestion, so we'll forget you made it.'

'All right. I'm asking you to let me do something which will take up none of your staff time. Just let me look at the firearms register for Aegina. That and the forensic report. It'll take an hour or two, then I'll hand them back. I can do it in this building. No disruption.'

Sotiriou seemed weary beyond endurance. 'You don't appreciate what your request means. I have to find those papers. That means putting someone onto it. I will then have to chase that person up, which will lead to further complications. If I'm seen to favour a particular case, it will create a precedent. I've been working for years to foster a culture of correctness in this department! The only way to achieve that is through self-discipline. I have to set an example, making no exceptions for anyone!'

George could hardly believe his ill luck. Another Bagatzounis! Clogging up the works with his 'correctness'. In a different context it would be admirable, but here it was delusional. The system was blocked. He was offering to unblock it, and these idiots were refusing him.

'Colonel, I understand your position. I wish every official in Greece had your honesty.'

'Don't try that on me. You don't wish that at all! And I hate flattery.'

'I'm not flattering you. I want you to see this from a different angle. You have a certain workload. It's too much for you. I'm offering to do some of it. I might even solve the crime. Wouldn't that be good?'

'We don't like outside help.'

'Why not?'

'If it's incompetent it makes things worse. If it's competent it makes us look bad.'

'So you don't want help?'

'Information yes. "Help" no.'

'OK,' said George. 'I'll give you information.'

'What information?'

'Anything useful I come up with.'

'Fine.'

'In exchange for an hour with those documents.'

'You're a cunning man, Zafiris.'

'I don't like the word "cunning".'

'It serves its purpose. I'll be cunning myself now. If you find the killer, I'm going to ask you to pass the name directly to us and no one else. Is that understood?'

George considered this. Before he could reply, Sotiriou went on: 'This is a test of your sincerity. If you want to help, you'll accept my conditions.'

'There's something I don't like,' said George.

'Tell me.'

'What happens if the information disappears into your system? If there's no arrest? Then I'll get the same story all over again.'

'I guarantee that will not happen.'

'How about a time limit?'

'What do you mean?'

'If there's no arrest within, say, two weeks, I can use the information in another way.'

'Two weeks is tight. Make it a month.'

'A month to make an arrest? That's ridiculous.'

'We have to check everything, prepare our case.'

'That takes a month?'

'It's not the standard time. We can often move faster. But I need a margin. And a permanent exclusion of press and media.'

'OK.'

'Leave it with me. Give me a number where I can reach you.'

George handed him a business card.

'Perhaps I could have a number for you, Colonel?' he said. 'A direct line?'

Sotirou considered this for a moment. 'Do you have a pen?'

'I do.'

George opened his notebook.

'This number is for your use only. Is that understood?'

'Of course.'

'Don't even write my name next to it in your book!'

'As you wish.'

He began spelling out the digits with terrible solemnity, as if they were nuclear codes.

12

George left the Violent Crimes Unit just after seven and walked slowly towards Leoforos Alexandras. The day's heat had faded, giving way to the voluptuous warmth of an early summer evening. Despite the obstructed pavements, the overflowing rubbish bins, the hooting cars, the sense of a city collapsing under its own bloated weight, he enjoyed the walk. Offices were closing, the bars and cafés filling up. He crossed Alexandras and headed towards Lykavittos up narrow streets scented with orange blossom. Something remained here of the old Athens, a grace that had been crushed out of the rest of the city by a fifty-year frenzy of building. He skirted the hill and cut through to Kolonaki. At Philippos, a restaurant he had not been to for years, he ordered a plate of roasted aubergines and a half litre of retsina.

He took *The Darkness of Ancient Greece* from his briefcase. Sipping the wine, he began to read. After a few uncontroversial remarks about classical Greek culture and its influence on the modern world, the first chapter described Plato's *Symposium:*

> *This conversation among friends is one of the founding documents of our civilisation – a debate about love and its place in human experience, set out in terms which have never been surpassed for drama, clarity and insight. No one disputes the status of this text as a masterpiece of Greek thought. At the same time, in*

a strange and disturbing case of attentional blindness, almost every reader ignores the true character of the society it represents – a society in which political repression, paedophilia, child labour, slavery, prostitution, and brutal wars of conquest are regarded as perfectly normal and acceptable; a society in which an intellectual giant – Socrates – could be forced to take poison for challenging the values of the ruling élite. As a Greek, I find it impossible to read this extraordinary dialogue without a pang of shame at the shallowness of our ancient 'democracy', and an even sharper stab of incredulity that it should have been so ignorantly worshipped, in Greece and elsewhere, for more than two thousand years. It is time we woke up from this irresponsible romantic dream…

George felt his anger rising. Like all Greeks he believed that somewhere in his nation's soul lay a deposit of ancient magnificence, a vein of gold that could mysteriously be mined, in moments of need, by every citizen of Greece. This was not "ignorant worship"! It was a certainty, based on facts! And there, to prove that greatness, was the Parthenon, just a few hundred metres from here, the world's most perfect structure, at the heart of Athens. That wasn't built on political repression and child labour! On paedophilia and slavery! Quite the opposite! It was the fruit of a vast community effort, a public subscription, in a city recovering from destruction by the Persian army. Not to mention the genius of its architect and sculptors, the skills of its stonemasons, its carpenters, its painters and labourers. It was rightly held sacred as a symbol of civilisation. Only a Greek who had abandoned his country could write such nonsense! If John Petrakis had stayed in

Athens, the daily sight of the Acropolis would have kept him wise and proportionate in his thinking.

Yet George found himself reading on, wondering what further outrages this iconoclast would commit.

He was interrupted in his reading by a call from Abbas asking if he planned to go to the memorial service for Petrakis. George hadn't been invited, didn't even know it was taking place.

'Don't worry about it,' said Abbas. 'Just be there.'

'Where?'

'Panagitsa Church, Aegina.'

'When?'

'Noon. Tomorrow.'

13

Next day at ten, he was on the ferry again, in a ragged, distracted state.

After the call from Abbas he couldn't sleep, so he stayed up late, drinking whisky, reading the professor's book. His mind was haunted by images of slaves digging out tunnels in the silver mines, women smeared with the blood of wild animals, boys and girls running naked under the Spartan sun, every face streaked with dust, sweat, and oil...

He bought a cup of coffee to combat his doziness and sat on the deck in bright sunshine as the sea breeze played about him. He watched an officer from the ship's crew make a crude attempt to pick up a blonde Scandinavian girl half his age. She was telling him to get lost, with little effect. George wondered if a couple of millennia ago the officer would have chosen a beardless boy.

When they reached Aegina, George hurried along the waterfront to the church of the Panagitsa. He lit a candle for the soul of the dead professor and took a seat at the back. The place soon filled up. Under the immense brass candelabra hanging from the dome, the memorial service began, the priests in their gold-embroidered robes swinging censers of fragrant smoke and chanting the liturgy with expressionless eyes. The friends and family of John Petrakis heard the tale of Lazarus raised from the dead and listened indifferently to the assurance that all humanity would put away corruption and rise in the love of Christ.

The service done, the congregation walked in pensive groups to Hippokampos, the little restaurant attached to the Hotel Brown. Trays of drinks and food were offered. George accepted a glass of cold white wine, and observed the people in the room. They were talking eagerly, like guests at a cocktail party. By the bar he spotted Abbas, who came over at once and asked him if there was anyone he would like to meet.

'You know them all?'

'Aegina's a small place.'

'OK,' said George. 'Start by the door. The lady with blonde hair and diamond earrings.'

'That's Regina Petrakis, wife of Constantine.'

'What do you know about her?'

'Too much. Only ten percent of his misery is innate, the rest is caused directly by her. How he sleeps at night is beyond me. She's a one-woman poison factory. The man she's talking to is Simeon Yerakas, with the silver hair and Italian suit.'

'What's his connection?'

'First cousin of Constantine. Behind him is…'

'I've heard the name before.'

'He's a property developer. Extremely well-connected.'

'Behind him?'

'Colleagues from various universities.'

'Any rivals there?'

'Every one of them!'

'I mean jealous rivals.'

'Mad enough to kill?' Abbas eyed him humorously.

'Why not?'

'I don't think so.'

'OK. Who else?'

'There's the Mayor of Aegina, and next to him, in that

appalling blue suit, is the president of the shopkeepers' union, Mr Kalamaras. Talking to him is the head of the secondary school, Mrs Frangopoulou. Then the man who runs the internet place by the school, Tzonis the butcher, Titina who owns the cinema, Costas the poet, Maria the herbalist…'

'Were they friends of John's?'

'They're all members of the Historical Society.'

'Unlikely to have murdered the man who was coming to lecture.'

'It would be a bizarre thing to do. Especially before the talk.'

George helped himself to another glass of wine from a passing waiter.

'Tell me, Abbas, have you read *The Darkness of Ancient Greece*?'

'Of course.'

'What did you think?'

'I enjoyed it. It's not quite the pioneering work that people claim – that was done years ago by scholars like Kenneth Dover – but it's a good synthesis of all that's known on the subject. And sharply written! That counts for a lot.'

'Who's Kenneth Dover?'

'He wrote the first modern investigation of homosexuality in ancient Greece. Speaking of which, here comes Bill.'

'Bill?'

'John's partner.'

George turned to see a muscular dark-haired man, forty-five years old, in a well-cut black suit. Abbas introduced them.

'I've been hoping to meet you,' said George.

'Why?' said Preston coldly.

'I'm trying to make sense of John's murder.'

'Aren't we all?'

86

'I know,' said George, 'but it's my job.'

'Police?'

'Private.'

Preston eyed him sceptically. 'Who's paying you?'

'Constantine.'

'I see.'

'I'd like to ask you some questions.'

'I was on the plane home when it happened.'

'You're not a suspect.'

'I should bloody well hope not! You never know in this lunatic asylum…'

'I need your help.'

'What do you want to know?'

'About rivals, enemies, any possible leads.'

'I won't be much help.'

'Maybe more than you think. Can we meet after this is over?'

'I'll look out for you.'

Preston moved away, stony-faced.

'What's his problem?' asked George.

'No idea,' said Abbas.

George surveyed the room, wishing he was anywhere but there.

'Who do you want to talk to now?' asked Abbas.

'I don't mind.'

'How about Yerakas?'

'He'll do.'

Abbas led him over. Yerakas was listening with a bored expression to a university professor who was machine-gunning him with words. The property developer saw them coming and turned away from the professor without a hint of apology. The professor stopped in mid-sentence, insulted and astonished.

Yerakas was cool and formal. They small-talked. George said he was surprised by the number of people at the memorial.

'John Petrakis was a famous man,' said Yerakas. 'There should be more people here. Where are the press when you want them?'

'Did you know him personally?'

'Of course.'

'Why "of course"?'

'He was my cousin.'

'Mother's side? Father's?'

'Mother's.'

'Were you close?'

Yerakas gave him a puzzled look. 'What do you mean by that?'

'Were you friends as well as cousins?'

'We played together as children. Then we led different lives.'

'So you're closer to Constantine?'

Yerakas did not answer the question directly. His eyes became noticeably colder.

'We've done business together.'

'Do you still do business together?'

'Why do you ask?'

'I was talking to Colonel Varzalis the other day.'

Yerakas nodded, an expression of boredom already veiling his face. 'I know who you mean.'

'I understand there has been conflict between you and the colonel.'

Yerakas grimaced slightly. 'That was years ago. Forgotten.'

'Not by the colonel.'

'I have no grudge against the colonel.'

'He stopped you building a hotel, is that right?'

'Temporarily.'

'What do you mean?'

'We found another site and built the hotel there. End of story.'

'On the island?'

'On many islands! Now you must excuse me, I was in the middle of a conversation with Professor Dimitriou…'

Yerakas turned back to the professor. 'You were saying?'

The professor continued smoothly, with a gratified expression, from the point where he had left off.

George found Abbas smoking a cigarette outside.

'Enjoy that?' asked Abbas.

'Oh yes. A beautiful conversation.'

'He and Constantine are great buddies.'

'Where's the hotel? The one they didn't build at the end of the colonel's garden?'

Abbas seemed unsure. 'They've built quite a few. Ever been to Perdika?'

'No.'

'Along the coast road, a mile or two before…'

George heard his phone ring. As he took it from his pocket Abbas spotted a friend and moved away.

'Hello? Zafiris here.'

'This is Colonel Sotiriou.'

George hurried out of the restaurant.

'Any news?'

'Good and bad.'

'Tell me.'

'I've located the firearms register for Aegina, and the forensic report.'

'Excellent. I'll come over tomorrow morning.'

'Unfortunately there's an irregularity.'

'Namely?'

'The numbers in the register are not continuous.'

'What does that mean?'

'A page has been removed. Neatly cut out. Approximately fifty weapons are unaccounted for.'

'It might still be useful.'

'Perhaps. But this constitutes a new crime. A second inquiry has been opened.'

'Is this related to the murder of Professor Petrakis?'

'We don't know.'

'Is there a copy of the register?'

'No. One day it will be computerised, but so far…'

'Can I come over and see it?'

'No.'

'Why not?'

'It has already gone to Kalamata, for analysis.'

'Kalamata, for heaven's sake! Why there?'

'I prefer someone outside Athens.'

George understood. It was a sensible precaution.

'How about the forensic report? Can I see that?'

'No.'

'Is that in Kalamata too?'

'It is.'

George thanked him and hung up.

This development was not good. Tracks were being covered, evidence destroyed.

He heard his name spoken sharply. Looking round, he saw Constantine Petrakis bearing down on him, his face furious.

'What the hell are you doing questioning Mr Yerakas like that?'

'Like what?'

'Is he a suspect?'

'Not at present.'

'So why embarrass him?'

'I wasn't aware of any embarrassment.'

'Mr Zafiris, I hired you to investigate my brother's murder. You've come to a private memorial service, uninvited…'

'I was invited.'

'By whom?'

'Abbas.'

Petrakis dismissed this contemptuously.

'I'm the one who invites you or does not invite you!'

'I don't see the problem.'

'You were not hired to pursue irrelevant inquiries at my expense! And certainly not to embarrass my guests at a private function!'

'I asked Yerakas about a hotel. He declined to discuss it. That's all.'

'Why did you ask Mr Yerakas about the hotel? What the hell has that got to do with anything?'

'Perhaps you might tell me.'

'What's that supposed to mean?'

'You know the story. I don't.'

'It's irrelevant.'

'It seems to cause a lot of anger.'

'Who told you about it?'

'Colonel Varzalis.'

'So you've seen him? Did you question him?'

'I did.'

'Did he make any sense?'

'A certain amount. His memory is patchy.'

'Conveniently patchy, I would say!'

'It seemed to cause him some distress.'

Petrakis nodded. 'He is a very skilful operator. Don't be

fooled! Have you asked him what he was doing on March 25th?'

'Not yet.'

'I suggest you do. And forget the hotel!'

'You think he shot your brother?'

'I'm not going to say what I think. But the man is a well known fascist. And a crack shot. I'm surprised you haven't confronted him.'

'He can't plan, he can't remember…'

'Who else have you talked to?'

'Abbas, Bagatzounis, Bill Preston, the head of the Violent Crimes Unit.'

'Four people? In a week?'

'I told you, there's no way of knowing how long this will take. I have other cases on the go. And the police are not being helpful.'

'That's why I hired you! To put a bomb under their arses! Now you need a bomb under yours!'

'The firearms register has been tampered with. Pages have been removed.'

'You know what? I don't give a damn! Either you have the balls for this job or you don't. I suspect you don't. I'm giving you three more days, then it's results or you're fired.'

'You're changing the parameters of the case.'

'To hell with the parameters of the case!'

Petrakis turned to leave, then swung back.

'And don't you dare talk to any more of my guests!'

Shaking with anger, George watched him go. He breathed deeply, struggling to stay calm. He was ready to walk away from this job. But not until he'd been paid.

14

Bill Preston found him still smouldering. 'Let's go somewhere else,' said the Englishman. 'I can't take any more of these idiots.'

They found a café on the waterfront. Preston ordered a beer, George a coffee.

Preston rolled a cigarette. He was flushed and angry, unsteady with emotion.

'What's going on?' asked George.

'What do you mean?'

'Something's upset you.'

'It's personal.'

'I'm sure it is.'

'So I'm not going to talk about it, all right? Just ask about John and leave all the rest.'

George let him simmer for a few moments.

'Would you roll me one of your cigarettes?'

Without a word Preston pushed his tobacco pouch across the table.

'I can't do it,' said George.

Preston shook his head disgustedly. He laid a cigarette paper on the table, lifted a pinch of tobacco from his pouch, began shaping and rolling. He licked the edge of the paper, smoothed it down, tucked in the strands of tobacco hanging from the ends with a match, and presented the sleek little tube to George.

'Thank you,' said George.

He was not a regular smoker. He just felt like a cigarette. And the raging energy on the other side of the table needed distraction. A few seconds of silence, concentration on a physical task, something outside his head... It might calm him down enough to talk without exploding.

Preston handed him the matches.

'There's a great deal about this case that people don't want me to know about,' said George. 'Things going on in the background. Family secrets, personal secrets, business secrets. I'm getting a sense of two brothers who didn't like each other very much. Am I right?'

'Constantine doesn't like anybody.'

'He likes Rosa Corneille.'

'Rosa's different.'

'Why?'

'She's a giver. A spiritual healer. Looks after him.'

'Does he need looking after?'

'Have you met his wife?'

'No.'

'When you do, you'll understand.'

'OK...' George paused. 'I'm trying to relate all this to John...'

Bill stubbed out his cigarette. 'OK, fuck it, I may as well tell you. John and I have a house on Mykonos. An old olive press. Did you know that?'

'No.'

'John bought it as a ruin. I rebuilt it, at my expense. That was my contribution. It's a lovely place. And it's worth a lot. Seven, eight hundred, something like that. Now Constantine's trying to get his filthy hands on it. Claims it's his – through his brother.'

'Is there any basis to that claim?'

'No. It's ours. Fifty-fifty. We agreed that.'

'That's on the title deeds?'

'No.'

'Mistake!'

'We were a couple. We shared everything.'

'Constantine disputes that?'

'Only the house on Mykonos. There's a house in London, but thank God he can't touch that.'

'He may be within his rights.'

'Bollocks. He's making it up. This is Europe. Doesn't matter if you're gay or straight, legally married or living together. You share the lot.'

'There may be some Greek variant on that.'

'He says there is. He's trying to frighten me.'

'Is he going to court?'

'Threatens to.'

'You must get a lawyer.'

'Do you have one in mind?'

George nodded.

'Would he talk to me? Tell me straight if I've got a case?'

'Of course.'

'Expensive?'

'Yes, but worth it. Won't take it on unless he's sure he can win.'

'How do I find him?'

'I'll give you his number.'

Bill took out a black notebook, opened it on a page covered with sketches. He turned a fresh leaf and wrote down the name and number.

'Tell me about the relationship between the two brothers,' said George.

'It wasn't healthy.'

'In what way?'

'They were totally different. John loved life. Loved art. Loved people too. Costa's got no time for that. For him it's money, status, and keeping up appearances.'

'That's not unusual in Greece.'

'Too damn right!'

'I meet plenty of people like him,' said George. 'They don't care about anyone or anything outside their own tight little circle of self-interest. Then, when things go wrong, they're surprised nobody wants to help them. So what else can you tell me?'

Preston thought about it. 'John was gay,' he said, 'Costa's straight as a bloody broom handle. And worried to death about the family name. Half the ancient Greeks were poofs, plus half the heroes of the war against the Turks – that was a book even John was scared to write! – but Costa couldn't handle that. A gay Petrakis! What will the neighbours think? And of course the neighbours all thought John was great. They loved him. That drove Costa crazy. He was freaked out by John, but envied what he had: friends, freedom, fame... John used to tell Costa to let go, but he couldn't, he was afraid everything would collapse if he didn't hold it all in his neurotic grip. Their father was the same. Couldn't move a muscle without worrying about how it might look. That was one good reason why John left Greece.'

'So John and his father didn't get on?'

'They sorted that out once he got to America. Status went up. Princeton beats gay.'

'What about Yerakas?'

'We never had anything to do with him.'

'Even socially?'

'Especially socially. John didn't like him. Didn't like the family generally.'

'Why did Costa hire me if they got on so badly?'

'Costa admired John. Maybe even loved him in his messed-up way. Always tried to get John to come back and live in Greece.'

'Why would he want that?'

'Keep the family together. But John wouldn't come. He loved London.'

'Did he love Greece too?'

'Adored it. For what it could be if…'

'If what?'

'If idiots like his brother weren't pulling all the strings.'

'I couldn't agree more.'

Preston nodded, smiled wistfully, looked away.

'What about Rosa?'

'I told you. She's special.'

'What's her role in all this?'

'She was a bridge between them.'

'Do you get on with her?'

'I'm not into this aura stuff.'

'Does Yerakas see her too?'

'Shouldn't think so. Too bloody full of himself.'

George watched Preston roll another cigarette.

'Do you have any idea who might have killed John?' he asked.

'Not a clue,' said Preston. 'It makes no sense.' His features were blurred by a cloud of cigarette smoke. 'On any level. It's just an insane, horrible thing… I wish I could help you more. Any more questions?'

'Not just now.'

'I need to get back to Athens.'

George gave him a card. 'Call if you get any ideas.'

'I will.'

Bill dug into his pocket and produced a card of his own. George examined it. *William Preston. Building. Design. Maintenance.* An address in south London.

'Don't take this the wrong way,' said George, 'but you seem unusually articulate and well educated for a builder.'

'Blame John for that.'

'How long were you together?'

'Twenty-five years.'

Preston was trying to smile, but tears flooded his eyes.

15

At the Café Agamemnon that evening, George met his colleague Hector Pezas. They sat in the shade, drinking beer, their voices loud among the empty tables.

Hector had been to see Mrs Boiatzis. 'She was pretty upset,' he said. 'She confronted her husband about his affair, threatened to leave him, go to the newspapers. They had a noisy row. He admitted having an affair with Mrs Kakridis, regretted it, agreed it was not the solution to their marital problems, promised to end it, and asked for forgiveness. She granted her forgiveness, or so she says, and he went off to the park. He was found dead a couple of hours later with a pistol in his hand.'

'Was it his pistol?'

'Apparently it was.'

'Apparently?'

'She thinks he owned a pistol, but she's not sure.'

'So we still don't know if he killed himself?

'Not a hundred percent.'

'How did Mrs Kakridis take the news?'

'I have no idea. And to be frank, I don't care. I'm pulling out. I've done what I was paid to do.'

'So have I,' said George, 'but Kakridis hasn't paid me yet.'

'Oh, big mistake! You told me to take the money up front,' said Hector.

'It was good advice. I should have followed it myself.'

They began discussing other business. George told Hector his frustrations over the Aegina murder.

'You're lucky to have the work,' said Hector.

'I'm turning stuff down.'

'Really? Like what?'

'Those four kids who died in the bank fire. During the May demonstrations.'

'I thought it was three.'

'One of the girls was pregnant, so that's four.'

'OK. So what's up?'

'The family want action.'

'I'll bet they do!'

'But I'm not going to do it.'

'Why not?'

'We're related. Family and business…'

'Pass them to me!'

'Are you short of work?'

'This crisis isn't exactly good for trade,' said Hector.

'Maybe it hasn't hit me yet.'

'It will… But you know what? Something in me likes this crisis. I thought the boom years were disgusting. Ever since the Olympics the whole country's been on a spending spree. Funded by what? Borrowing! Just one long bout of self-indulgence, with prices shooting up and nobody giving a damn. They just went on spending. Now we're paying for it. As we should. I welcome the austerity. The country needs it. But my business doesn't need it!'

'We did well for a long time.'

'Didn't we just! All those selfish people trying to get dirt on other selfish people, with plenty of money to spend. Now they're counting their pennies. They don't feel the need for us any more.'

'All the professions are suffering. Even doctors and lawyers.'

'At least there's that. Earn a million, declare ten thousand. Bastards.'

'Do you declare everything you earn?'

Pezas stopped in mid-flow.

'Do you?' George insisted.

'No more than you do,' said Pezas, nonplussed.

'So why blame doctors and lawyers?'

'It's the amounts! The shamelessness! The pretence of being ethical professions. That's what sticks in my throat.'

'But the principle's the same. We all cheat, but we want others to be punished.'

Pezas laughed. 'What do you expect? That's the Greek way!'

'It's infantile. We have to grow up.'

'Will you lead the way?'

'I'll think about it.'

'I'm sure we all will!'

Pezas stood up. 'I must go. Let me know if you get any more work you can't handle.'

'I will. Actually there is something you could do for me. Half a day's work.'

'Sure. What is it?'

'Research on a businessman, Simeon Yerakas.'

'What do you want to know?'

'His family and business interests.'

'Anything in particular?'

'No, the whole thing. But I'd be particularly interested in any business connections with a man called Constantine Petrakis.'

'You want him followed?'

'No. Just the information. Half a day's work. No more.'

'Understood.'

George climbed the stairs to his apartment. He was tired, but he had one more thing to do before he could rest.

He picked up the telephone to Antonis Mihalopoulos, his lawyer, and recounted Bill Preston's difficulties with Constantine Petrakis. The lawyer bristled when he heard the name.

'I'd prefer not to get tangled up with that family,' he said.

'Why?'

'They hire the best.'

'I thought you were the best.'

'I'm as good as the best,' said Mihalopoulos.

'That will do nicely.'

George told him what he knew. Mihalopoulos said he would talk to Preston.

'OK,' said George. 'One more thing. What can you tell me about Simeon Yerakas?'

'He's not involved, is he?'

'No.'

'If he is, stay away.'

'Why?'

'Just take my word for it. He's a man to avoid.'

'I met him today.'

'Lucky you. Just don't let him think you owe him a favour.'

'What do you mean?'

'He has a way of making life impossible for his enemies.'

'How?'

'He takes the game away from them, fills the horizon with trouble.'

'You're talking in metaphors.'

'That's all you can do. You turn up for a game of tennis against Yerakas, and you find the courts have been sold for development and you're arrested for trespassing. Suddenly you're dealing with the police. Are you sure Yerakas isn't after Preston's land?'

'I don't know. He has some joint ventures with Constantine Petrakis.'

'Let's hope this isn't one of them. If it is, you can tell Preston it won't be worth the fight.'

16

The telephone rang the next morning as George was shaving. He ignored it and finished the job, taking his time, using soap, brush and razor, running the blade carefully over the angles of jaw and throat. This was a good moment of the day, not to be hurried, although the mirror sent back a merciless account of spent years. At last the ringing stopped.

He dried his face, pulled on a clean shirt and walked through to the kitchen to make coffee. The telephone started ringing again.

It was Abbas. 'I've got something for you,' he said.

'What?'

'A list of gun owners in Aegina.'

'Where did you get it?'

'The colonel.'

'How did he come by it?'

'He compiled it.'

'When? '

'Eight years ago. It's a list of his defence volunteers.'

'Is it still valid?'

'It's a place to start. In fact I've checked the list. There are three names in the right area. If you come over, we could go and talk to them.'

George considered this. He had only a short time left.

'I can be there in a couple of hours.'

'Excellent. I'll meet you at the ship.'

Abbas was standing on the quay as the ferry backed in. 'You made good time,' he said. 'We'll get a cab over there.'

'Sorry, what's the cab for?'

'I'm going to show you the hotel.'

'Which hotel?'

'The Aegina Palace. So-called!'

'I didn't come to see a hotel.'

'It won't take long. And you need to see it. You may not think so, but you do.'

George checked his watch. It was just past noon.

'How long?' he asked.

'Half an hour.'

They found a taxi and drove south along the coast, passing a series of small resorts – beach umbrellas and bars tucked in between the road and a narrow strip of sand. A few swimmers bobbed offshore, their heads black in the silvery glare.

'The island's not famed for its beaches,' said Abbas.

'So why did Yerakas build here?'

'Wait till you see what he built!'

They passed a placid bay shaded with eucalyptus trees, where half a dozen speedboats rested at anchor. A few hundred metres further on, the taxi driver pulled over, pointing straight ahead.

'That's it,' he said.

George peered through the windscreen at an enormous U-shaped block, six or seven storeys high, in reinforced concrete, once painted white, now a dirty grey. It looked like an abandoned prison.

'That can never have been attractive,' said George.

'Correct!'

'How long did it stay in business?'

'Five years.'

'Damn stupid thing to build there!'

'Damn stupid thing to build anywhere! But that's the Yerakas style. Put up something monstrous, stick it in the brochures of travel companies in northern Europe, where people sit miserably through the winter, dreaming of the Mediterranean sun, then watch the cash roll in.'

'It must work or he wouldn't do it.'

'It worked in Corfu, it worked in Crete. They have airports and big sandy beaches. Aegina's different. It's not for the hordes. No airport, and you've seen the beaches. To get here those frozen northerners needed (1) a flight to Athens, (2) a bus to Piraeus, (3) a ship to Aegina, and (4) a bus to this place. That's too much like hard work.'

'He should have known that.'

'He should indeed. But he was determined to do something in Aegina. Leave his sign, like a dog marking territory. A hotel in town might have worked, but the colonel stopped him.'

'He and Constantine must have lost money here.'

'And who did they blame? Not their own stupidity, not their greed, but an old soldier trying to protect the architectural heritage of his island.'

'There must be more to it than money,' said George.

'You misjudge them,' said Abbas. 'They only see money. It's the whole story to them.'

'And so they try to get Varzalis condemned for murder? That doesn't make sense.'

'And what in Greece does make sense?'

Abbas's eyes were fiery with anger.

'Maybe there's another motive,' said George.

'Such as?'

'Maybe they know who did it.'

'That needs thinking about,' said Abbas.

He leaned forward and told the taxi driver to go on to Perdika. Then he turned back to George.

'Swim? Lunch?'

'How about the list?'

'I'm coming to that. You say "maybe they know who did it". That's an intriguing thought. But why would Constantine hire you to investigate if he knew who did it?'

'He just told me – as good as told me – my job is to dig up evidence against the colonel!'

Abbas considered this. 'That's a whole new category of twisted,' he said.

'It's called revenge,' said George.

'OK, but if someone killed my brother, I'd want the right man put away!'

'You would. So would I. But we're dealing with a strange man.'

They rode along in silence for a while. The taxi slowed down.

'This is Perdika,' said the driver. 'Right or straight on?'

'Go right,' said Abbas. 'I need to get my head under water. It's too damn hot to think right now.'

'And the list?' said George.

Abbas flashed him a slightly deranged smile. 'You'll see the list.'

They plunged off the rocks into deep water, then stretched out in the sun to dry. Refreshed at first by the coolness of the swim, they soon felt hot and light-headed again.

'There's only one thing for it,' said Abbas. 'Another swim, then lunch in a shady taverna.'

George said, 'Listen, Abbas, I'm not going another step

until you show me that list. You dragged me over to the island on that pretext and now I'm starting to think there's something else going on.'

'I just wanted to slow you down to the right pace.'

'If I slow down any further I'll be asleep!'

'OK! Now we're getting somewhere!'

'No! You're trying to lead me somewhere. That's a different matter.'

'I'm only trying to lead you to a taverna. Where you can consider this thing in its true perspective.'

George stood up. 'Forget it. I'm going back to Athens.'

'To do what?'

'Get on with my life!'

'You're making a mistake.'

'I don't care. I don't have time to piss about.'

Abbas dipped his hand into his trouser pocket. 'OK,' he said. 'This is not quite the moment I had chosen, but never mind.'

He handed over two folded sheets of paper.

George opened them. Typewritten names and addresses, some corrected in blue ink, each marked with a cross, an X or an asterisk. Addresses in Aegina or Angistri. At the top of the first sheet was the word ΕΘΕΛΟΝΤΕΣ. Volunteers. A note on the second sheet explained the symbols:

* = rifle

+ = pistol

x = shotgun

'Did the colonel give you this,' asked George, 'or was it already in your possession?'

'The colonel gave it to me.'

'You told him it was for me?'

'Of course.'

'Did he remember me?'

'No.'

'So how did you explain it?'

'I told him the story from the beginning. The murder, the investigation, and so on. He has just enough memory to hold onto the essential facts.'

George thought about this. It could still be an elaborate trick, but the chances of that were getting slimmer. Who would go to the trouble of cutting a page from the firearms register and then provide a handmade substitute? Unless the substitute itself were designed to throw the police off the trail?

'I have one troubling thought,' said George.

'What's that?'

'The colonel's failing memory. It seems strangely selective. It's a powerful argument for his innocence, because this crime, and the subsequent cover-up of evidence, require forethought, which in turn requires a functioning memory. But there's a problem. There are many problems. For a start, how did he remember the existence of this list?'

Abbas did not answer the question. Instead he asked a question of his own: 'What cover-up of evidence?'

George replied cautiously. 'That's confidential. The details don't matter. Can you answer my question?'

'The colonel didn't remember the list.'

'How did it come to light?'

'I remembered it.'

'You remembered it? How?'

'The way one does! You asked me about the firearms register, I thought of the colonel's list, I went and asked him if he still had it, he said he had no idea, so we went through his files.'

'That still leaves me wondering how you came to know of

109

its existence in the first place.'

'That takes us back,' said Abbas. 'Nearly ten years.'

'To what?'

'2001. I remember the conversation clearly. The colonel and I were on the ferry, returning from a rifle-club meeting in Athens. It was that day of infamy when the World Trade Center was destroyed. The televisions on the ship – things I detest normally – were just announcing the news.'

'What time was this?'

'Around six in the evening.'

George worked it out. Nine a.m. in New York, plus an hour or two for the news to get out, plus seven hours difference. The time was right. 'Go on.'

'The colonel was horrified. It seemed to strike right down into his soul. He was also impressed by the efficiency of the terrorist attack, viewed as a purely technical accomplishment. He could see the logistics behind it, of course, being an expert himself.'

'Expert in what?'

'Counter-terrorism and intelligence.'

'I didn't know that.'

'That was his field.'

'OK. Go on.'

'I think not,' said Abbas.

'Why?'

'This is not the place for it, out here on the rocks. I'm roasting alive. Why don't we go and get settled in a taverna down the road there, get a flask of retsina, and then I can tell you this story properly?'

'I don't like these delays.'

'OK, suit yourself. We'll sit here and I'll make it short. And in the usual Athenian way you'll miss the point because you're in too much of a hurry!'

'I have just two more days to close this case.'

'Says who?'

'Says my client.'

'Tell him to go boil his arse.'

'I would very much like to. But he's paying.'

'OK. I'm offering you the chance to meet three men who possess the right kind of weapon, in the right place, to have shot Professor Petrakis. Do you understand that?'

'I do.'

'I want to tell you about these three men. But I don't want to do it while my balls get grilled on this block of limestone. I might miss a crucial detail. Are you still with me?'

'I need to work quickly.'

'No, my friend, that's your big mistake! You are in a rush and it's doing you no damn good at all.'

'This is an investigation! I ask the questions and move on!'

'OK, go and see these guys yourself. Leave me out of it.'

'Which ones are they?'

'Paraskevás, Kotsis and Tasakos.'

George scanned the list. All three had asterisks, meaning rifles. He could go and see them himself. It would take time to find them in the warren of back streets, and he would have to interview them cold... He wondered why Abbas was so determined to do things at this slow pace. To have lunch, spin things out?

'All right,' he said. 'We'll do it your way. But I need a timetable.'

'Five minutes swim. Five to the restaurant. One hour for lunch. Fifteeen minutes drive back to town in a taxi which we will book now. Half an hour for each interview. Ten minutes de-briefing. That's three hours. You'll be on the 4.15 ferry back to Piraeus.'

'OK. It's a plan at least. Let's try and stick to it.'

With the retsina on the table in front of them, and the aromatic smoke of grilling sardines rolling out of the kitchen window, Abbas continued his tale of that evening in 2001.

'The colonel was filling in the background for me – the logistical steps that those terrrorists would have had to take in order to hijack five aircraft simultaneously and fly them at those targets. He laid it all out as if he'd conceived it himself. The pilot training, the organisational network, the coded communications by phone and email… We discussed it on the ship from Athens, and went on far into the evening back at his house. I asked him how well defended Greece would be against such an attack, and he gave me the answer you'd expect: very poorly indeed. But, he said, there are informal defence corps, groups of volunteers who could make themselves available in a national emergency, like they did in the Second World War. I was cynical about that, I remember, because Greeks don't generally like to put themselves out for the collective good. He was stung by that. He showed me his list of armed volunteers. Waved it in front of me, to prove that there's still some decency and fight left in the old country. I was perfectly willing to take his word for it, but he was determined to prove his point. He made me read it. Name by name.'

'Were you drinking?'

'You bet we were! Kyra Sophia brought us meatballs and cheese at some point because she didn't like to see us boozing on empty stomachs.'

'Did you often drink together?'

'We weren't in the habit. But when the time came, when the mood took us, we went at it hard.'

'I'm surprised he told you about the volunteers.'

'Why? Because I'm a foreigner?'

'Yes.'

'We're friends. Nationality doesn't matter a damn.'

'Except in times of war.'

'OK. But Persia was last at war with Greece in 330 BC. We've never found a reason to fight again.'

'Do his volunteers still meet?'

'No. Stopped about five years ago.'

'What did they do?'

Abbas smiled at the memory. 'We got together on Wednesday evenings. In winter we had classes in subjects like the handling and placing of explosives, urban and guerrilla warfare, communications, defence planning, organisation and supply, even "military strategy from Alexander the Great to Ho Chi Minh". In the warmer months we were active. Shooting, fitness, rock-climbing, unarmed combat, manoeuvres, simulated attacks on fixed and moving targets, survival in the wild, seaborne invasion – it was a full military training in miniature. God, we had some laughs!'

'Varzalis ran the whole thing?'

'We had guest speakers from time to time, but all the action was led by him.'

'You took it seriously?'

'Yes and no.'

'What do you mean?'

'You had to take it seriously or you were out. Varzalis demanded commitment. And he got it. But at the back of my mind there was always a sceptical voice saying, "Come on, this is just a game!" Only of course games have to be taken seriously to be enjoyed. So I had a double consciousness, maybe even a triple consciousness.'

'You've lost me. Why triple?'

'The first is serious, the second sceptical, the third an awareness of both. And I suppose the fourth is the awareness of the awareness, but that's a little too curious for a hot afternoon.'

George wondered how Abbas could ever get anything done with a brain like that. 'Was that just you playing mind games,' he asked, 'or others too?'

'I never enquired. But you know, when we were in action it was totally absorbing. For an academic like me, who's spent his life in libraries and lecture halls, it was exhilarating. I remember one night, half of us were detailed to defend an old German gun battery overlooking the sea, while the other half attacked it. I was in the defence group. It was terrifying. We knew an attack was coming, but we didn't know when, or from where. I witnessed an impressive and highly unexpected fact about human perception. A figure standing still in the landscape is invisible. Invisible, I tell you! Especially at night. It's only movement that catches the eye. A man can be standing just a few feet away and you'll fail to see him. The mere knowledge of that is frightening. And the night is enormous! Full of strange noises, mysterious shapes and movements. Where among all those shadows, those pools of ink, is your enemy? Beside that olive tree? In that ruined house? Or behind you? I had no voice at the back of my mind then, I can tell you! Only fear and excitement that lasted till dawn. I still have goose pimples now when I think of it.'

'You had weapons, I presume?'

'Only knives on that occasion. Not real ones, of course. You had to get your opponent at a clear disadvantage, then you won.'

'So the rifles were a side issue?'

'On that exercise, yes. On others we used them, either with blanks or with live rounds for target practice.'

Abbas seemed lost in his memories. 'We wouldn't have been able to do much in reality, but we were well trained, and we'd have given the enemy a few headaches. We respected the colonel totally.'

'All of you?'

'Every one.'

'Have you remained friends?'

'Mostly. Some drifted away.'

'Was there anyone among you who had any disagreements with the colonel? Or was maybe humiliated by him?'

'It wasn't his style to humiliate. He spoke bluntly, but never cruelly. His mind was always on the mission. Criticism always for a good reason.'

'He made no enemies?'

'Not in our group.'

'Anywhere else?'

'You're asking me these questions as if Varzalis had been killed rather than the professor!'

'There's a chance he will be if this murder is pinned on him.'

'There's no death penalty in Greece.'

'Just the living death of a prison sentence.'

Abbas nodded. He turned his gaze to the sea, where a small fishing boat was entering the harbour, seagulls flitting along its wake. 'I just hope it never happens to him. Or, if it does, that he dies first...' He turned back to George. 'Tell me, why are you interested in the volunteers?'

'They intrigue me.'

Abbas seemed amused.

George glanced through the names again. 'Tell me about

these three you mentioned, Kotsis, Paraskevás and Tasakos.'

Abbas described them to him: a retired policeman, a pilot with Olympic Airways and a man who owned a couple of shops in town. All, in his opinion, steady, honest, law-abiding people, without grudges, fanatical opinions or mental instability.

'So why would any of them choose to shoot Professor Petrakis?'

'That's the big question!'

The sardines arrived, with a plate of fried potatoes and a salad of tomato and cucumber. Abbas ordered another half litre of retsina and checked his watch. 'If we're sticking to the timetable, we've got twenty-five minutes to eat these,' he said.

'It's OK,' said George. 'I'm starting to think you're right. Let's take our time.'

17

They called first on the pilot, Paraskevás. A solidly built man in his forties, he explained that he had sold his rifle four years ago when his son was born.

'I didn't want any weapons in the house with children around. You can lock your guns away as carefully as you like, but children are curious. They find keys. They explore.'

George asked him what kind of gun he had owned.

'A Winchester 70,' said the pilot. 'A collector's piece, inherited from my father.'

'Was it registered with the police?'

'Of course.'

'Who bought it from you?'

'A farmer from Souvala. Do you want his name?'

'And his address.'

'I don't think I wrote it down. His name was Koromilás.'

'What do you know about him?'

'Not much. He seemed a normal farmer. Big hands, hairy, sunburnt. Drives a pick-up truck.'

They talked briefly about one of the great economic riddles of the day: the dwindling sums that farmers were paid for their produce and the ever more bloated prices in supermarkets. Someone was making grotesque profits... George let the conversation ramble, watching the pilot talk. He seemed relaxed, not hiding anything. He wished them luck with their investigation.

Next they called on the retired policeman, Evangelos Kotsis. He had clearly been woken up by the doorbell, but he welcomed them sleepily in, and asked his wife to make coffee. They sat in his yard, shaded by vines, attended by bees, admiring his prolific vegetable garden: melons, tomatoes, peppers, aubergines, and, a little further off, orange and lemon trees, the fruit small and sharply green among the leaves. Pots of geraniums and lilies clustered around the table where they sat.

'Not bad for a town garden,' said Abbas.

The old man nodded. 'You have to do something when you retire. Otherwise what's the point?'

The scent of lilies was reminding George of his friend's funeral, while the manic fullness of the garden brought to mind the nightmare of Sotiriou's office in Athens. He watched the old policeman rubbing his eyes and asking what he could do for them.

'My friend is investigating the Petrakis murder,' said Abbas. 'Up there in that window we can just see. You're on the list of gun owners in this area. So Mr Zafiris would like to see what weapons you have and ask you some questions.'

'What sort of questions?'

'Where were you on the night of the murder?'

'Date?'

'March 25th.'

'I'll fetch my diary.'

'And your rifle!'

He was back a few minutes later, in company with his wife, who asked him worriedly what he wanted with the gun.

The policeman explained, and handed the weapon to George.

'Take a look,' he said. 'It's not loaded.'

George examined it. World War Two by the look of it.

'Is this a Nazi symbol?' He pointed to a tiny eagle and swastika stamped into the metalwork near the trigger guard.

'That's right. A captured Wehrmacht weapon. Used by guerrillas in the resistance. Given to me by my uncle.'

'What is it? A Mauser?'

'Correct. Karabiner 98K.'

'What do you use it for?'

'Hunting.'

'In Aegina?'

'No. Epirus.'

'What do you find up there?'

'Deer, wild boar, mountain goats.'

'Enough for hunting?'

'Oh yes. Plenty.' He winked. 'Especially if you get lost and cross the Albanian border.'

'Can you remember where you were on March 25th?'

'I'll tell you exactly.'

Kotsis opened his diary, flipped back a few pages, studied one of them closely, and said, 'I was in Ioannina. Staying with my cousin Angelos, son of the uncle who gave me the Mauser. The next day we went hunting.'

'Did you have this gun with you?'

'I did.'

'Is it registered with the police?'

Kotsis gave him a stern look. 'It certainly is.'

'Can I have the telephone number of your cousin?'

'Of course. Have you got pen and paper?'

George took down the number.

'Call him in the evening. He's out on the land during the day.'

George shut his notebook. He felt the man was solid. No

119

reluctance there. Little point going any further, but he would try one last question.

'Since the murder was committed, someone has been at the firearms register and cut out a page. Do you know anyone in this neighbourhood who is capable of getting into the local station and tampering with the evidence in that way? Maybe a relative of one of the officers? Or a friend?'

Kotsis looked blank.

'Because whoever cut that page out is almost certainly the killer.'

Kotsis nodded thoughtfully, but said no more.

'Thank you,' said George. 'I won't take up any more of your time.'

Their last stop was the internet shop, CosmoWire, where they found the proprietor behind a glass partition separating him from a darkened room packed with computer terminals. At each of these sat two or three boys, their faces lit by the changing images on the screens. A strange, jumbled soundtrack of car engines, explosions, gunshots, groans and frenzied music strung an invisible mesh through the air, which was hot and rancid with adolescent sweat. The boys' eyes were intently focussed on the games. Some were excited, others playing with a cold expertise that George found unsettling. The man in charge asked them what they wanted.

'I'm looking for Manos Tasakos.'

'What for?'

'I need to ask him a few questions.'

'About what?'

'I'll explain when I see him.'

'Are you an inspector of some kind?'

George gave him his card.

'I see,' said the man, handing back the card. 'What do you want to know?'

'Are you Mr Tasakos?'

'I am.'

'I understand you possess a rifle.'

'No longer.'

'What happened to it?'

'I gave it away.'

'When?'

'Four or five years ago.'

'Do you remember the manufacturer's name?'

'Mauser. '

'Old? New?'

'At least fifty years old. Maybe older.'

'What did you use it for?'

'Shooting birds, targets… Normal things.'

'Where were you on the night of March 25th this year?'

The man reached for his mobile phone and started pressing buttons.

'March 25th? In Athens all day.'

'Did you stay the night?'

'No. I came back on the last boat.'

'What time was that?'

'Seven? Something like that.'

'What were you doing in Athens?'

'Business.'

'Did you meet people?'

'Of course.'

'People who could vouch for your presence there?'

'Yes.'

'What sort of business were you doing?'

'Buying computers.'

'For this place?'

'No. Another one.'

'Same kind of thing?'

The man nodded. 'An internet facility.'

George gave him a sceptical look. 'Is that what you call it?'

'You have a problem with it?'

'I don't like to see kids stuck in front of computers.'

'It's the work-station of the future.'

'I know. But children should be doing more wholesome things.'

'They're safe in here. With two parents at work all day, someone has to look after them.'

'No doubt. But that's not what I'm here to talk about.'

'What are you here to talk about?'

'Professor John Petrakis.'

'Oh.' The man's expression changed. 'That was a sad business.'

'Sad indeed.'

'Of course everyone knows who did it.'

'Do they?'

Tasakos glanced at Abbas. 'You've heard of Colonel Varzalis?' he said.

'I have. I can't see why he would do it.'

'He's lost his mind. No reason at all. Just ping! Dead man.'

'I understand he's a friend of yours.'

'That's true.'

'Don't you feel bad accusing him?'

'I'm not accusing him. I'm just telling you what a lot of people are saying. If you didn't hear it from me you'd hear it from someone else. And of course I feel bad. Only he'll never be charged.'

'Why not?'

'He has connections. Right to the top. Even if they try him, and find him guilty, he'll never serve a prison sentence because he's old and ill.'

Tasakos took a cigarette from a packet on his desk and lit it.

'Can I get you a coffee?'

George thanked him but said he must get back to Athens. They walked out through the thudding twilight of the shop into the street's bright glare.

'What do you think?' asked Abbas as they took the harbour road.

'How well do you know Tasakos?'

'So-so.'

'Weren't you volunteers together?'

'Yes. He's a good man. Has a lot of worries, though. A difficult life.'

'In what way?'

'His wife's a recluse, and very obese. The son's not much better.'

'Just one child?'

'There's another son in Germany. But he keeps his distance.'

'He's prickly about his business.'

'You weren't exactly diplomatic. And he gets a lot of criticism. No one likes to see kids under the spell of those violent games. Fantasy it may be, but it has an effect. It has to.'

'Anyway,' said George, 'it's irrelevant. He doesn't own a gun, and he was in Athens all day. If all three men are telling the truth I'm no further forward.'

'If!'

'I now have just one day left.'

'You need to see that forensic report.'

'Damn right I do! And suppose it says the gun was a

Mauser? We have two! How many of those are there on the island?'

'Quite a few. The Germans had millions of them.'

George thought about this. It didn't help.

'I'd better catch my boat,' he said.

18

George reached home in the early evening. He was expecting his son Nick from London at ten, and wanted to tidy up before he arrived. The place was a mess. He gathered the old newspapers and magazines from the sitting room, stuffed the dirty clothes from the bedroom floor into a laundry basket, washed up the dirty plates in the kitchen, and went quickly round with a hoover and duster. His head was bursting. Abbas was right. He needed to slow down.

Just after eight he received a message to say the flight was delayed by two hours. A bomb alert at Heathrow. 'Don't wait up, Dad. See you in the morning.'

There was still work to be done. He took a can of beer from the fridge and opened up his laptop.

The first thing he saw was an email from Pezas with the results of his research on Yerakas. He read it slowly, twice. Yerakas had built hotels, apartment complexes and marinas all over Greece, choosing his locations skilfully. The Aegina Palace seemed to be a rare error. He also had interests in shopping malls, golf courses, water supply and sewage treatment. There were ambitious plans for an 'eco-apart-hotel' to be built on a nature reserve, currently on hold because of the country's debt crisis.

'GOOD!' Pezas had written alongside this last part.

Yerakas was married, with two daughters and a son. He also had a brother and a sister. The brother worked in Zurich in investment banking. The sister was married to a businessman in Athens. She had one son.

George called Pezas. 'Thanks for the report,' he said. 'Thorough as usual. But there's a name missing.'

'Which one?'

'You say Yerakas has a sister married to a businessman in Athens. What's his name?

'Hell, I knew you'd ask. I didn't get that.'

'Why not?'

'I was interrupted, and couldn't get back to my informant.'

'Can you find out for me?'

'Not right away.'

'Why not?'

'I'm having drinks with a friend.'

'After drinks?'

'It's a lady friend.'

'You should have said! Call me in the morning.'

He put down the phone, thinking with amusement of Pezas, one of the horniest men on the planet, having drinks with a 'lady friend'. Still playing the field at forty-five. Still thinking of sex every three minutes. Tomorrow he would either be grinning with a conqueror's pride or crippled with existential doubt. Did I move too fast? Am I losing my touch? Maybe she's the other way? George had talked him down after a few such encounters. It was like being twenty again, with that feeling of half the human race enveloped in the deepest, most impenetrable, most beautiful mystery…

He was hungry, and ordered kebabs from a takeaway. He tidied his desk while waiting. When the doorbell rang he opened up, gave the man his six euros, went back into the sitting room with a second can of beer from the fridge, and settled down to eat.

He needed to think a little about the next few days. Nick was scheduled to go to Andros in the morning, and he wanted to go with him, but he also had to make his report to Petrakis. There would be no time to write it tomorrow. He would have to do it tonight, even if it was inconclusive, with crucial information missing. But that was the price Petrakis paid for being a shit and in a hurry.

He was tired. In former days he would have lined up the beers, the cigarettes, the songs; lamp on, music on, typewriter loaded with paper and carbon. Then go at it like hell. Till any hour of the night. Till dawn if necessary. Now he just felt like going to bed.

He crumpled the kebab box and dropped it in the bin. Then he pulled the ring on the can of beer, thought nostalgically of the Papastratos cigarettes he used to smoke, and opened the laptop.

Two hours later, it was done. He printed the report, signed it, scanned it. He emailed the scan to Petrakis, and tucked the original into a folder on his desk. He stood up, arched his back, and checked his watch. Half past ten. Nick would be here at midnight. He wanted to be up to see him, not asleep on the sofa like an old man in front of the TV. He decided to go out for a stroll.

19

As soon as he got in he knew something was wrong. A smell of tobacco in the hallway, lights on all the way up the stairs. He ran up and found his door open. Dimitri stood on the landing looking appalled. Thieves had got in and pulled everything from his study shelves, emptied cupboards and drawers, flung books and papers across the floor.

'Did you see anything?' asked George.

'I heard a few noises,' said Dimitri. 'I wanted to come and check, but Tasia wouldn't let me.'

'She was right.'

'How did they get in?'

George checked the door.

'Probably a credit card. I didn't double-lock.'

Dimitri offered to help clear up. George said no, he could handle it. 'Go to Tasia. You need to be with her.'

He checked the other rooms. They were untouched. But the study was thoroughly ransacked. The laptop had gone from the desk. The old French wooden wine cases where he kept his cameras and audio equipment had been cleared. He checked the desk drawers. These had been searched, and a few items were missing: memory sticks, a portable hard drive, his Beretta. The files on the desk had been taken too.

The doorbell rang.

Nick was standing on the threshold next to a big suitcase.

They embraced.

Nick said, 'You look shattered.'

'I'm fine,' said George. 'How was the bomb scare in London?'

'Very calm and British. It was nothing as it turned out.'

Over his father's shoulder Nick saw the study. 'Hell, dad, what's happened here?'

'I've just had a break-in.' George felt suddenly weak. 'I need to call the police, make a list of stolen things…'

'Do the list in the morning. You should rest now.'

'You're right,' said George. 'But let's have a whisky first.'

Over a glass of Talisker they talked. Nick spoke about his course, his friends, his girl, the rivers of beer that irrigate student life. He found it miraculous that people could study and pass exams with so much booze in their blood. 'What's the secret? They get drunk at night, then up the next morning, breakfast at eight, lectures at nine. Hung over, feeling like hell, but in there, like clockwork. It's a system. And it runs very smoothly.'

'While the Greek drinks only coffee and fights his way through chaos every day.'

'And what a surprise, we're in crisis.'

'Maybe it's the breakfast that does it,' said George.

'Breakfast, a cold climate, and thinking as a community.'

'We invented that, for God's sake, and we've forgotten it!'

'Did we really?' said Nick. 'Isn't it found in all human societies?'

'Found and sometimes lost,' said George pensively. He stared into his glass.

'Let's hope we can find it again,' said Nick, raising his. 'Cheers!'

They drank to their hopes. 'A lot will depend on your generation,' said George. 'You can see how it works in England. Bring it back here. Don't compromise.'

'I could say the same to you,' said Nick. 'You studied abroad, you saw it. What happened?'

'That's a damn good question,' said George. 'The answer is just one word: PASOK.'

'Really? How about two words: New Democracy?'

'OK, both parties are to blame. One sat complacently on the old order, the other broke it up and made things worse. But for me, PASOK was the killer. Andreas Papandreou was a clever man. Taught economics at Harvard, as you know. He wanted Greece to be a more equal society. He began well, helped the poor, built hospitals, said all the right things. Then the power went to his head. He bought votes with money from Europe, created the most bloated, obstructive bureaucracy on the planet, and nationalised the best of Greek industry, transforming it from a source of income and jobs to a drain on national resources. He poisoned this country! Wrecked the economy and destroyed all hope for the future in the space of ten years!'

'And you expect us to fix it?'

'No. Of course not. You can't. Just don't make it worse.'

'That's a hell of a legacy,' said Nick. 'I'm not sure I want it.'

'It's yours anyway,' said George. 'Make the best of it.'

He poured another drink, adding a little water to the whisky.

George asked what they were saying in London about the Greek crisis.

'Oh, the usual stuff,' said Nick. 'The Greeks are lazy and corrupt. They spend all day in cafés and on the beach, and never pay their taxes. You hear it all the time. It's pretty offensive.'

'What about the economy?'

'They say we'll have to leave the euro. Devalue, make exports cheaper, fix the deficit.'

'No one says that here,' said George. 'Even if it's the obvious answer.'

Next morning, sipping strong coffee after a late night, George tried to marshal his thoughts. All his working material was missing. Some archives too: three boxes of press cuttings, one of photos. All electronic storage devices, including the back-up copies he had made of essential files. His phone and diary, his weapons. He was going to have to spend the next few days repairing the losses.

Where should he begin?

He remembered the colonel's list of volunteers. He made a note to call Abbas, hoping he had made a copy.

The telephone rang.

'Mr Zafiris?'

A voice he did not recognise.

'Who's speaking?'

'How are you feeling?'

'Who's speaking?'

'Stay out of other people's business.'

'Tell me who you are, so that…'

The voice interrupted him. 'There won't be a second warning.'

The line went dead.

George swore. Threatening calls were standard. But these stupid shits could never see beyond their own noses. Whose business was he supposed to stay out of?

He reached for the telephone directory, looked up Kakridis, Petrakis and Pezas, and jotted their numbers down. He rang Kakridis first, got an answering machine and left a message.

Next he tried Petrakis.

'Yes?' The unmistakable, suspicion-filled voice.

'Zafiris here. I have a question and I want a straight answer.'

'Go ahead.'

'Did you send someone to raid my flat last night?'

'Why would I do that?'

'Perhaps you might tell me.'

'I did not.'

'I've also had a threatening phone call.'

'What do you want me to do about it?'

'If it was you that instigated it…'

'I don't do that kind of thing.'

'Or some agent of yours?'

'Absolutely not!'

George wondered what else he might ask. His head was hurting, his mind working slowly.

'Is that all?' asked Petrakis.

'Well, since we're talking, did you receive my email?'

'I did, and I replied.'

'My computer's gone, so I haven't read your reply.'

The voice hesitated. 'Wait one second. I'll read it to you…
Thank you for your report. I need to consider the matter carefully before committing any further expenditure. Please regard this investigation as closed and forward to my office all relevant paperwork.'

'Closed?' George could not hide his disappointment. 'You really want me to stop?'

'That is the usual meaning of the word.'

'What paperwork do you want?'

'Everything. I wish to weigh up all the evidence you have gathered and think it through for myself.'

'My office has been ransacked. I don't know what I'll find.'

'Just send me what you've got.'

'If the job's closed, I may as well send you my invoice too.'

'Very well. My office will deal with it.'

George sat at his strangely uncluttered desk and stared at the list of things he had lost.

Having stared for a while, he decided he had better do something about it. He telephoned the local police station. The duty officer must have been in a good mood, because rather than giving him the usual brush-off he promised to send someone round.

When Nick appeared for breakfast, George asked his advice on finding a new mobile phone and computer. Nick said he was happy to look into it. That was two things done, or at least started. Progress.

The telephone rang.

'Good morning,' said an energetic voice. 'Colonel Sotiriou here.'

George told him about the burglary, the lost files and equipment.

'I wish they'd visit my office,' said Sotiriou.

'If I see them again I'll tell them.'

'OK, listen, Zafiris, I have a favour to ask you.'

'Go ahead.'

'You're aware of the death of a member of parliament last week?'

'Boiatzis.'

'Correct. Did you know him?'

'Not personally.'

'I understand there was some kind of *ménage à quatre* going on with his wife and another politician, whose name I shan't mention.'

'Where did you hear that?'

'Never mind where I heard it. Your name has also come up in relation to this. What can you tell me?'

'It sounds as if you know as much as I do. Who's your source?'

'I'm not going to tell you that, so stop asking.'

'Was it Pezas?'

'You didn't hear what I said.'

'What exactly do you want to know, Colonel?'

'I want to know what you know. How long these affairs went on. How serious they were. Whether there could be any connection between them and the death of Boiatzis, or whether there was some other motive, financial, political, personal, which led him to shoot himself or to…' Sotiriou stopped abruptly.

'Or what?'

'Or not.'

'Is there any doubt about it?'

'There's no doubt that he died.'

'Is there any doubt that he shot himself?'

'Stop asking me questions. I'm asking you! And by the way, you're obliged to answer. I can charge you for withholding evidence.'

George described his dealings with 'the other politician', not mentioning his name, trying hard to be dispassionate. This was tricky.

Sotiriou at once said, 'He sounds like a monster.'

George refrained from comment. Instead he asked, 'What do you plan to do?'

'I'm not telling you my plans.'

'No of course not. How foolish of me to ask.'

Sotiriou thanked him brusquely for his help and rang off.

The next thing George should have done, he later realised, was call Kakridis. But that was something he never did willingly. Instead, he calculated his bill for Petrakis.

It was simple enough. Seven days at 320 euros: 2,240. Six return trips to Aegina: 120. Taxi and metro fares: 30. All his receipts had gone, so he had to guess these. He would not charge for telephone calls or extra hours.

He wrote out a fair copy, folded it into an envelope, and was about to call Petrakis for his office address when the telephone rang again. It was then he realised he should have called Kakridis. The minister was already shouting before George had raised the instrument to his ear.

'First I get some shitty message about men in motorcycle helmets, as if I'm a bloody gangster. Then it's the police asking me about my love life! And all of this can only have come from one person: you! If this is your way of blackmailing me for a fee that you are now in no position to claim, I have just two words to say: fuck off!'

'I'm not blackmailing you, Mr Kakridis.'

'Oh no? That's funny because it feels just like being blackmailed, and you'd better be aware, Mr Detective, that what I do to blackmailers makes them regret the day they met me.'

'I am not blackmailing you, sir. There's no connection between any of this and your failure to pay me.'

'Bullshit.'

'Bullshit to you!'

'You messed up the job and now you're trying to force me to pay.'

'I gave you the information you asked for.'

'And then you gave it to the fucking police!'

'I did not.'

'How did the police find out?'

'I have no idea.'

'It had to be you!'

'It was not.'

'Who else then?'

'I tell you, I don't know. It could be anyone. A journalist? Maybe your wife herself? Wives know a great deal more than…'

'Don't lecture me on what wives know! Someone talked to the police. I gave you clear orders to keep this thing quiet…'

George felt his temper flaring. He struggled to control himself.

Kakridis roared on, 'Today the police, tomorrow the press!'

'I'm not your public relations manager, Mr Kakridis.'

'You can say that again! You're a fucking blackmailer!'

George was ready to slam down the phone. But Kakridis would be hoping for that.

'I've sent you my invoice,' he said calmly. 'You have thirty days to pay it, then my lawyer takes over.'

'You're going to need a damn good one!'

'I pay my bills, Mr Kakridis. It saves me a lot of trouble. I suggest you do the same.'

'Go fuck yourself.'

'Have a nice day,' said George, and replaced the receiver.

Horrible as that last call had been, he now had to pick up the phone again and speak to Pezas. If his friend was leaking stories to the police, he might also be leaking them to the press, either directly or indirectly.

'Hector? Listen, I want you to be straight with me. Did you talk to the police about Boiatzis and Kakridis?'

'No. Why?'

'They're onto it.'

'Which section?'

'Violent Crimes.'

'For a suicide?'

'There's a hint it may not have been suicide.'

'Who called you?'

'Sotiriou.'

'Oh!'

'Do you know him?'

'He's an old friend.'

'He knew about the love affairs. I thought you might have told him.'

'No way.'

'Do you swear that, Hector?'

'On my life.'

'OK. I'm going to believe you. New question. Have you found that name for me?'

'Which one?'

'The man married to the sister of Simeon Yerakas.'

'Shit, I forgot.'

'Too busy with your lady friend?'

'Sort of.'

'Is your brain now permanently located between your legs?'

'I'm sorry, George. I'll make this a priority.'

'Do that, because I've got something else for you.'

'Namely?'

'I want you to watch my back for a few days.'

'That's an expensive job.'

'I know. Have you got anything else on?'

'Nothing pressing. What's up?'

'You'll give me a good rate?'

'The best.'

'Which is?'

'Don't ask.'

'I need to know. Kakridis isn't paying me and Petrakis has pulled the plug on the Aegina job. So things are tight.'

'Just pay me what you want.'

'OK.'

'George, why do you need me to watch your back?'

'I've been threatened.'

'Seriously?'

'That's how I'm taking it. I'll explain when I see you. I want to nail these guys, but I can't do it on my own. One more thing. I need a good pistol. Compact and reliable. Do you have a spare?'

'What do you normally use?'

'Beretta 950.'

'I've got one. When do you want me to come over? Today? Tomorrow?'

'Any time. I'm not going out.'

In the afternoon, Zoe telephoned to ask how he was feeling. He told her he was fine.

'Nick's worried,' she said.

'I know. He doesn't need to be.'

'I want you to come to Andros.'

'Maybe at the weekend.'

'I want to know you're safe.'

'Don't worry.'

'How can I not worry?'

'Hector's going to watch the place.'

'That's not enough.'

'Listen, Zoe, they took what they wanted. They won't be

back.'

'But you're having the place watched.'

'It's just a precaution.'

'I don't know how you can be so calm.'

'I have to be, that's all. '

She said no more. She seemed frustrated and hurt.

'There's something else,' she said. 'I've spoken to Anastasia's family.'

'About what?'

'The fire in the bank.'

'Oh…'

'They're willing to pay for a private investigation.'

'Why not wait for the police?'

'You know why.'

'I'm not doing it.'

'Why not, George? The money's there!'

'They'll want it done cheaply.'

'Just tell them what you charge.'

'They'll still want a discount. It'll get messy, believe me.'

'They'll be offended.'

'That's how the mess begins. Just say I'm too busy.'

'It's not an answer, George! They're desperate!'

'I'll ask Hector.'

'They'll still wonder why you won't do it.'

'Zoe, please respect my judgement. I'm telling you this is best kept outside the family!'

Angrily, she hung up.

20

Pezas arrived at nine the next morning. He snapped open his briefcase, took out a Beretta 950B and a box of ammunition and set them down on the desk.

'Same model as mine,' said George. 'Only in better condition.'

'It's a spare.'

'Can I buy it from you?'

'No. I want it back.'

George pushed the gun to one side.

'What else, Hector?'

'I've got that name for you.'

'Which name?'

'Yerakas's daughter married a man called Tasakos.'

Tasakos. The name rang a bell, although he couldn't quite place it.

'Isn't the case closed now?' asked Pezas.

'I have a feeling it's going to open up again.'

A hard look from Pezas. 'Is anyone paying you?'

'Not right now. I'm hoping Petrakis will think again.'

'If he doesn't?'

'Then I'll have to think again.'

'What about Kakridis?'

George threw up his hands. 'He's gone crazy. But he'll have to pay me at some point.'

'I meant, what about him and Boiatzis?'

'Sotiriou thinks there's something going on.'

'Then there probably is.'

'Who's paying for your time on that one?' asked Pezas.

'Nobody.'

'Then do yourself a favour, George, and stay out of it!'

'I'll try.'

Pezas was restless, ready to leave. George asked him if he would be interested in the bank job. Pezas said sure, if they could pay. Then he said, 'I should get to work. What do you want?'

'Check if I'm being followed. Look out for danger.'

'Who's after you?'

'Maybe you'll tell me that.'

Pezas glanced out of the window, at the church garden opposite, the street climbing the hill.

'I'll take a walk around. What are you doing today?'

'Phone calls, a little shopping, putting my life back together.'

'Fine. Let me know when you're going out. I'll be down in the café for the next half hour if you think of anything else.'

The day had grown hot and he wanted to sleep. He lay down in the bedroom, gazed at the bars of light that filtered through the shutters, heard the canary next door singing, the distant traffic sounds, and let himself drift away.

Next thing he knew the telephone was ringing.

'Hello, George! Abbas calling.'

He mumbled a sleepy greeting.

'I hope I didn't wake you up. I have some bad news about my friend Colonel Varzalis.'

'What's that?'

'He's been arrested. For the murder of John Petrakis.'

'On what evidence?'

'I don't know. Kyra Sophia has just come round to tell me. She's in a dreadful state.'

'You know I'm no longer on the case?'

There was a pause. 'What's happened?'

'Constantine pulled the plug.'

'Did you send in a report?'

'Of course.'

'May I ask what you said about the colonel?'

'I said I believed him to be innocent.'

'Can you come over and talk to the police?'

'What good will it do?'

'They might release him.'

'On my word? No way.'

'His health is not great, you know. Greek police cells are nasty places.'

'Listen, Abbas, I'm in a tricky position. Unpaid. And I don't do voluntary work.'

'I understand. Would you be prepared at least to telephone the police?'

George considered it. He could not very well refuse. 'I'll do that,' he said.

'I'm going to see the colonel now,' said Abbas. 'I'll keep you informed.'

He rang off.

George made a cup of coffee and steeled himself to call the police in Aegina. This was not going to be pleasant. He was put through to Captain Bagatzounis.

'Are you acting as attorney for Colonel Varzalis?' asked the captain.

'No, I'm acting as...'

'I can only speak to his legal representative!'

'I'm speaking to you as a concerned citizen.'

'I can only speak to his legal representative.'

'You've arrested the wrong man.'

'I repeat: I can only speak to a legal representative.'

'OK, if you can't speak, you can listen. There is no way Colonel Varzalis committed that crime. You've been fed false evidence by people who want to damage him.'

'I have his confession in front of me.'

'His what?!'

'I have a confession, signed by Colonel Varzalis.'

George attempted to take this in.

'Are you satisfied, Mr Zafiris?'

'I'll call you back.'

He rang Abbas and told him the news.

'That's preposterous,' said Abbas. 'He would never have written such a thing.'

'Ask him when you see him. If it's genuine we might as well give up hope.'

'Of course it's not genuine!'

'Then we have to find the person who faked it.'

'The old man won't know if he wrote it or not.'

'Ask him anyway. And find his lawyer, so you can get him out on bail.'

'I'll do that. Stay in touch.'

The news about Varzalis distressed him. The missing information from the firearms register and the forensic report were now more necessary than ever. No one could bring John Petrakis back to life, but every day the colonel spent in prison, or under the shadow of arrest and trial, would undermine his health, adding fresh injustice to old.

He telephoned police headquarters in Kalamata.

'Forensic department please. Takis Mitropoulos.'

Takis came straight onto the line. 'How can I help?'

'Somehow, please, get your hands on the forensic report on the Petrakis shooting, and let me know what it says.'

'It should be in Athens.'

'No. It's somewhere there, in your department. Sotiriou sent it over.'

'Funny place to send it.'

'Why?'

'We're moving into new offices. Everything is in packing cases.'

'I don't believe it! How long can a removal take?'

'Weeks, apparently. The new building isn't ready, and the contractors haven't been paid so they're going slowly. Meanwhile this building has been sold for development and the new owners are pressing for completion before the tax increases on property purchases come into force next month. So half our stuff is in boxes, the other half in a warehouse somewhere.'

'How do you get any work done?'

'With difficulty.'

'Can you have a look for that report?'

'I'll try, but no promises.'

George put down the phone. His head was buzzing. There were obstructions everywhere. And questions. Why had Sotiriou sent the files to an office that was moving? Had he known that, or was it an unlucky accident? And why had Varzalis 'confessed' to the shooting? Had someone fooled him into signing it? Or forged his signature? Or was it genuine? And why the hell was he thinking about all this anyway – unpaid?

It was time for coffee at the Agamemnon. If not the cure for all ills, at least it reduced the pain. He sat in his usual place and nodded to Dimitri. He reached for the newspaper.

The headline shook him. "MURDER!"

Underneath was a photograph of Boiatzis.

A smaller headline elaborated: "Boiatzis did not take his own life". The caption under the photo read, "Murder victim or suicide? The death of MP Angelos Boiatzis is the subject of frenzied speculation. Full story, page 3."

Curious, thought George, how this startling claim of murder was quickly watered down to "speculation". The headline was there to sell the paper, the caption to prepare the reader for the more subtle truth, which was… what? He turned to the article on page 3.

A radio journalist, Sophocles Ghiotis, had asserted that Boiatzis was murdered. He had privileged information, he said, which he was prepared under certain conditions to share with the police. The motive for the killing was discoveries made by Boiatzis about "dirty dollars in the construction industry – bribes, sweeteners, hush money paid to politicians, civil servants, planning officers, building inspectors and auditors." Boiatzis had been preparing a dossier on the subject for personal submission to the Prime Minister. The article did not say what had happened to the dossier, but Ghiotis promised to reveal more in the coming days.

He turned to the next page. There was a photo of the bearded Ghiotis, headphones on a balding head, a sharp, pale, humourless face. Ghiotis ran a radio station, Paranoia FM, which had a cult following. It specialised in irreverent, hard-hitting exposés of scandal in politics, sport, business and the media. George did not care for the face of the man, but he warmed at once to the project.

Dimitri brought his coffee.

'Have you heard of Paranoia FM, Dimitri?'

'No. What is it? A comedy show?'

'Radio station.'

'Never. Ask your son. He'll know.'

George returned to the paper. The other big story was a strike by dock workers that had stopped passengers on cruise ships disembarking in Piraeus. The cruise companies were now threatening to cease visiting Greece. An editorial ranted at the folly of strikes that endangered tourism, 'our country's lifeblood'.

A movement caught his eye. Pezas had appeared.

'How's it looking?' asked George.

'Clear so far.'

'Have you seen the paper?'

'Only the headline. What's the story?'

'A radio journalist says Boiatzis was killed.'

'What's his evidence?'

'He hasn't said yet. I'd like to talk to him.'

'And who's paying you to do that?'

'No one,' said George.

'Forget it.'

Pezas ordered coffee. 'By the way,' he said, 'why were you so keen to get hold of the name of Yerakas' son-in-law?'

'Just being thorough.'

'Did it ring any bells?'

'No. I've heard the name before but now I've lost my files I can't remember where the hell I met or heard of the man.'

'Recently?'

'I think so.'

'Aegina or Athens?'

'If I knew that it would help.'

'Are you on the case again?'

'Emotionally yes. Financially no. Colonel Varzalis has been arrested, probably on a false confession. It's just possible he shot the professor but my guts tell me he didn't.'

Pezas was thoughtful, his blue eyes looking hard into George's. 'You want to help Colonel Varzalis?'

'I'd like to.'

'Get him to pay you.'

'While he's in prison?'

'That's the best time! He'll be keen to get out.'

'Remember,' said George, 'he and Petrakis dislike each other. I can't see him paying good money to look into the death of his enemy's brother.'

'He needs to clear his name.'

'Why the hell should the innocent pay to clear their names?'

'I agree,' said Pezas. 'It's a crime. But what choice does he have?'

'I'm not going to suggest it.'

'Why not?'

'Come on, Hector! It makes me look like a bloody vulture.'

'Get your friend Abbas to suggest it.'

'That's not a bad idea.'

'Varzalis has money, right?'

'Seems to.'

'There you are. You'll be doing him a favour. Go for it and stop worrying.'

Dimitri brought coffee for Pezas, who leaned back in his chair and surveyed the street with a critical air.

'What are you going to do now?' asked George.

'Go back to the office,' said Pezas, 'deal with some paperwork. There's nothing happening here. Dimitri will keep an eye out. I've briefed him. He's got my number.'

'Can you come back later? After dark?'

'If you like.'

'Your lady isn't making demands?'

'No. She's off to Milan this evening.'

'Working?'

'Shopping.'

'Sounds like an expensive woman.'

'Prices are twenty percent lower there. She says we're being robbed over here. For everything. Food, clothes, household goods. So much for the benefits of a European currency!'

'Still, add the air fares and the hotel…'

'She stays with friends, and the air fare is peanuts.'

George raised his hands. 'She's obviously a model of thrift and globalisation.'

'That's what I like about her,' said Pezas. He drained his coffee. 'And the fact that she goes like a train…'

He stood up. 'I'll come over at ten tonight.'

'Fine. By the way, did my wife's cousin call you?'

'She did. That's what I'm going to make a start on now. Strike while the iron's hot.'

He waved and was off down the hill.

21

That afternoon, as he was opening the day's post, a call came through from Colonel Sotiriou.

'I've just heard from your friend Mr Kakridis,' he said.

'A great honour,' said George flatly.

'An honour maybe,' said Sotiriou, 'but not a pleasant experience.'

'It rarely is. What was the subject of your conversation?'

Choosing his words with care, Sotiriou replied: 'Kakridis has accused me of political motivation… and taking bribes from his enemies.'

'Is any of that true?'

'Of course not!'

'Then forget about it.'

'I find that difficult.'

'Kakridis specialises in unjust accusations, close to the bone. This puts you on the defensive, and distracts you from your purpose.'

'I'm sure that's right…'

Sotiriou was silent again. Uneasy. George wondered what was on his mind.

'Is there anything else?' he asked.

'No,' said Sotiriou. 'I just wanted to know your thoughts.'

'Have you heard about Paranoia FM?'

'Only what I read in the paper this morning.'

'Have you had any contact with this Sophocles Ghiotis?'

'None at all.'

'You don't have any files on him?'

'Why should I?'

'He's a leftie.'

'That's not a crime.'

'I thought the police liked to watch people of alternative political persuasions.'

'I certainly don't.'

George wondered whether to believe him.

'I have news from Aegina,' said Sotiriou. 'Colonel Varzalis has been arrested.'

'I heard,' said George.

'We have a confession. It's a big step forward.'

'I believe the confession to be false.'

'How do you know that?'

'I don't know. I said I believe. The reason is simple. There is absolutely no motive.'

'I understand that he and the Petrakis family have had conflicts in the past.'

'The colonel with Constantine Petrakis. Not with John.'

'That's still a motive.'

'Not in my book. Varzalis doesn't hate Petrakis. He doesn't give a damn about him.'

'How do you know that?'

'He told me himself.'

'Colonel Varzalis is also mentally unstable.'

'He's suffering from Alzheimer's. He is not mentally unstable.'

'His brain is diseased.'

'You're being very crude, Colonel. The main symptom of Alzheimer's is memory loss. Not mental instability.'

'Some patients show both. I've done my reading, Zafiris!'

'Some patients, yes. Not all. Colonel Varzalis is perfectly stable. He's not violent or moody.'

'Psychiatric tests will reveal the truth.'

'I hope so. And I hope the psychiatrists will talk to his housekeeper, who lives with him and sees the situation from day to day.'

'No doubt they will.'

'But the inescapable fact in all this,' said George, 'is his failing memory.'

'Agreed.'

'He can't remember what happened five minutes ago! How the hell can he remember what he did on 25th March? Can you explain that?'

Sotiriou took his time to reply. 'I understand your frustration,' he said, 'but the due processes must be allowed to take their course.'

'The forensic report and weapons register are stuck in the middle of an office move in Kalamata! Is that part of the due processes?'

'That is unfortunate.'

'And why is Colonel Varzalis under arrest? He's not going to run away! Why has Bagatzounis accepted the authenticity of this confession without asking the most obvious question about it? Why does the convenience of the police prevail over a man's rights? A sick man at that! Where are the due processes there?'

'I'm sure Colonel Varzalis has a lawyer.'

'So?'

'He'll get bail.'

'I hope for the sake of your conscience he does!'

'Be patient, Mr Zafiris. Take it easy.'

'That's a phrase I particularly dislike. It's the motto of

every lousy waster in this country who can't be bothered to do his job properly, or consider the rights of another human being. Taking it easy is the national disease!'

'I couldn't agree more. But in your case, a bit of relaxation wouldn't hurt. I've learned the hard way what happens to people who don't know how to let go. Heart problems are just the beginning!'

'All right, Colonel. Fair point. But you need to know the police are committing an injustice here. A terrible injustice. And I'm not going to let you get away with it.'

'We'll see who gets away with what,' said Sotiriou with an air of menace, and ended the call.

22

Aristotle Street lay on a fault-line in Athenian society, which George crossed several times each week. To the west, Exarchia, the university district, its shabby, once elegant buildings sprayed with black graffiti promising death to bankers and politicians. Men with pony-tails and beards, girls in pre-ripped jeans and Indian blouses. Cannabis and alternative cafés, with stencilled heads of Marx, Lenin and Che Guevara adorning walls and doorways. To the east, separated by an invisible barrier, a line in the air, lay Kolonaki, with its luxury apartments and shops, where the debt crisis was still something people read about in the newspaper over a five-euro cappuccino. Here lived the old moneyed families of Athens – the lawyers, professors and technocrats, the financiers and politicians denounced on the streets of Exarchia. Rivers of kinship and money ran between the two districts, deep underground. On the surface they were as different as could be. Walking between them, George sometimes wondered how they could exist side by side.

He and Zoe had studied abroad, and they feared for their son's future if he joined Exarchia's festival of unreality, so they had sent him to university in England. He would have a shock if he ever returned to work in Greece, but the way things were looking, with half the country's youth unemployed, that was unlikely. At least he would absorb some of the civic ideals of northern Europe. Fairness, transparency, equality of opportunity, consonance of word and deed, impartial enforcement of the law – these to Nick would be realities, not fairy tales for the ignorant, to be aired at election time then cynically set aside.

George worried about the future of his country. With its corrupted institutions, its confused habits of thought, its cynicism and despair, it needed a great statesman to lead it out of its trouble. A Lincoln, a Churchill, a Mandela. Failing that a Venizelos, or even a Trikoupis. There was no such character in sight. Only equivocators in suits.

Most of all he worried about the next generation. Fodder for the advertisers, the propagandists, the exploiters. And no jobs for them! No hope! He was haunted by that computer game parlour in Aegina, where the present as well as the future was dark.

As soon as he got in, the telephone rang. It was Takis from Kalamata. He had found the forensic report.

'What gun was used, what ammunition?' asked George.

'Heckler & Koch G3. Israeli bullet, 12 millimetre.'

'Israeli? What's that about?'

'Doesn't mean much. They're big manufacturers.'

'How many shots?'

'Just one, through the window. Sniper's accuracy. They give an angle of entry: 25 degrees left of centre lateral anterior, 15 degrees vertical.'

'What does "left of centre" mean? Centre of what?'

'It doesn't say. Presumably the mid-line of the skull.'

'OK, I'm writing all this down.'

'Find the gun and you're in business.'

'Without the firearms register that's going to be hard.'

'I'm looking for it.'

'Can you put this information in writing for me?'

'Why?'

'I'm dealing with some awkward people here. I want to have something official to show them.'

'You want me to lose my job?'

'Sorry?'

'This is all unofficial. I'm not supposed to see these reports. Certainly not reveal their contents to outsiders.'

'I understand. You've been very kind.'

'Don't mention it. And I mean that literally.'

'Of course. Stay well, Taki. See you soon.'

At once he called Abbas.

'Ask the colonel if he's ever owned a Heckler & Koch G3.'

'Why?'

'I can't tell you why. Please just ask him.'

'You can speak to him yourself.'

'Are you with him?'

'In the prison. What a shit-hole! Waiting for his lawyer to show up.'

'OK. I'll talk to him.'

George put the question directly to the colonel.

'No,' came the reply. 'It's an effective weapon, no doubt about that, but not my kind of thing at all.'

'Why would anyone in Greece use Israeli bullets?'

'Why not? They have to be made somewhere.'

'Could the gun be ex-army?'

'Of course.'

'I mean ex-Israeli army.'

'Why not?'

'Do you know anyone in Aegina with a G3?'

'There was one, I believe. But who?'

'Maybe one of your volunteer force?'

'Could be. I don't remember.'

'It could help you get out of prison if you remembered.'

'My forgetfulness is the worst prison there could be.'

'I'm sorry, Colonel. Thank you.'

'That's quite all right. I don't know who you are, but you're welcome.'

Abbas came back on the line.

'Helpful?' he asked.

'Possibly. It's still the word of a man with a failing memory.'

'I asked him about employing you. He wants to know how much you charge per day.'

'Three hundred.'

'Hold on.'

A few moments later he came back.

'He offers two.'

'Tell him no.'

'What's the minimum you'll take?'

'Three. A week in advance. And it's not negotiable.'

'Tough terms of business!'

'There are reasons for that.'

'Obviously. Give me a moment.'

He could hear them discussing the matter in low voices.

'George? The colonel finds your price very high, and prefers to handle this matter himself.'

'That's fine. Wish him luck. He'll spend ten times that amount on his lawyer.'

'No doubt.'

George rang off with a pang of regret. They were just starting to get somewhere now, but, unless he was paid, every minute he spent on this was lost time.

23

Pezas had been watching his place since ten that evening. At a quarter to eleven he called.

'A motorbike has just pulled up,' he said. 'Two riders, in leathers and helmets, and they're letting themselves into your building. Do you have any bikers living there?'

'No.'

'I thought not.'

'What shall I do?'

'Is the Beretta loaded?'

'It is.'

'Let them in, but plan it. Take no chances. Show them who's boss. We need to talk to them.'

'Are you coming up?'

'I'm on my way.'

George picked up the Beretta. He did not want to let these people in, and wondered if Pezas was right about talking to them. They did not sound like talking types.

He stood by the door, rapidly thinking out how this should go. He needed to surprise them, get the upper hand at once. But he needed to get behind them, and he didn't want shooting. Before he was ready, the doorbell rang. He put his eye to the spyhole, just before a gloved hand flew up to cover it. The bell rang again. George waited. He wanted Hector there. Even with a Beretta in his hand, it was two against one.

He heard voices on the landing. Pezas had appeared. He was challenging them. One of the men spoke back angrily. Pezas insisted. Again the angry reply, and a shout of alarm.

George pulled the door open. One of the men had pushed Pezas against the far wall and was going at him with a heavy stick. Pezas was crowding him, denying him room, but he took some hefty blows to his arms and shoulders. The other man, hearing the door open, wheeled round to face him.

'Drop the stick!' said George.

The attacker didn't move.

'Drop the stick, I said! Or I shoot!'

A sudden movement to his left made George switch his attention. He caught sight of a knife blade moving swiftly towards him, and twisted to his left to see his shirt sliced open, quickly followed by a line of blood. The hand and blade flashed past, halted for an instant, and quickly swung back for a second stab. George pulled the trigger. The gunshot rang explosively in the confined space. The man sank with a groan.

'Don't move or I'll shoot again!'

The injured man was clutching at his leg, the knife on the floor, blood-slicked.

His eyes darting from one to the other, George said, 'Put that stick down or I'll shoot you too.'

The second man did not budge.

George took a step forward and fired at the man's right shoulder, jerking him forward onto Pezas, who disgustedly writhed away, dropping him to the ground. Pezas grabbed the man's left arm and stuck a foot in his back.

Neighbours began opening doors above and below.

'What's going on?'

'We have intruders in the building,' said George. 'They're under control. I'm calling the police.'

He had blood trickling from his stomach.

Dimitri's door opened. His tired, worried face peered out, taking in the scene with astonishment.

'Are you OK, George?'

'I'm fine.'

'You're bleeding.'

'It's superficial.'

'Who are these people?'

'I don't know.'

'Do you need a hand?'

'I wouldn't mind.'

George grabbed the right arm of the man close to him and twisted it back, forcing his head to the floor.

'Get the helmet off,' he said, 'if you can.'

Dimitri wrenched at the helmet while George kept the arm pulled round hard. The head that emerged was flushed and sweating: a balding man in his thirties, with a black goatee beard, a powerful beak of a nose and angry green eyes.

'Do the other one too,' said George.

'OK.'

As Dimitri put his hands on the helmet, the man inside it began to writhe like a scorched snake. Pezas kicked him in the side and he stopped. Dimitri eased the helmet off. They saw a round, puffy face, cropped red hair, dark with sweat.

'Who are you?' asked Pezas.

There was no answer.

Pezas repeated it, louder.

'Do you think they understand?' asked Dimitri.

'We'll find out,' said Pezas. He placed his foot on the redhead's wounded shoulder and pressed down. The man yelled with pain.

'Who sent you?'

The man said nothing.

Pezas thrust his foot down again.

'Who sent you?'

The man muttered something unpleasant in a language they did not recognise. He was weeping with pain, slobbering onto the floor.

'They don't speak Greek,' said George.

He emptied their pockets. In one he found a pistol of a type he had never seen before, a star in a circle embossed on the handle. Ten rounds of ammunition, a few euros, cigarettes, a lighter, chewing gum, mobile phone. No identification papers. In the other he found a different brand of cigarettes, a lighter, a flick-knife and the keys to the bike.

'We'll take them inside,' he said.

'They need a doctor,' said Dimitri.

'That can wait.'

'Tasia can take a look. She should look at you too.'

'OK, but first let's get them in and find out who the hell they are.'

George kept his Beretta trained on them while Pezas and Dimitri helped them into the flat.

'In the kitchen,' he said.

They sat the men on chairs. George gave the black-haired one his phone and said in English: 'Call your boss.'

The man pointed to the spreading bloodstain on his thigh.

'Later. First we talk to your boss.'

With a resentful look the man found a number and called it. He began to speak. His voice sounded tired. George took the phone from him.

'Listen,' he said, 'I've got your two bikers here and I'm not letting them go until I know who the hell I'm dealing with and what you want.'

'Fuck you,' said a voice. The line went dead.

'Fuck you too,' said George quietly and pocketed the phone.

'Time to call the police,' said Pezas. 'They have interpreters, they'll know what to do with them.'

'I'll get Tasia,' said Dimitri.

Pezas held the gun on them while George called the police. He reported the incident as an armed assault. He could already foresee problems – shooting in self-defence would lay him open to serious counter-charges. He added that he was wounded, afraid, and needed help at once. He gave the address and asked how long it would be.

'Is this an emergency?' asked the policeman.

'Of course it's an emergency!'

'Are the armed men still on the premises?'

'They are. But we've managed to disarm them. They're injured and they'll need medical attention.'

'So you're not in immediate danger?'

'I don't know how much danger I'm in. I've been stabbed in the stomach. And these bastards may have back-up. I need you to come now!'

'OK, fifteen minutes.'

When he returned to the kitchen Tasia was there, bathing and bandaging the men's wounds.

'They need to go to hospital,' she said. 'This one's lost a lot of blood.'

She indicated the dark one, whose face was pale and drained of energy.

'I've called the police and told them he needs a doctor,' said George.

'Who shot them?' she asked.

'I did.'

She did not ask why.

'Do you know who they are?'

'No. They don't speak Greek. Maybe a few words of English.'

'I don't like these people,' she said.

'I didn't invite them, I promise you.'

'Let me see your wound.'

George lifted his shirt. She examined the cut with expert fingers, cleaned it with cotton wool soaked in alcohol, and laid a piece of gauze over it.

'Hold that for me,' she said, and cut four lengths of sticking plaster.

'You were lucky this didn't go any deeper,' she said.

'I know.'

'Change this dressing every 24 hours.'

She packed away her bottle of alcohol, cotton wool and spare bandages in a cloth bag.

'Thank you, Tasia. I'm sorry about all these disturbances.'

'It's all right, George. I'm not completely useless yet.' She smiled sadly. 'I'll go now. Stay as long as you like, Dimitri. As long as they need you.'

A few minutes later the police arrived. A young officer who introduced himself as Lieutenant Kassavitis, and a junior. Neither looked older than twenty-one.

George explained the situation. Kassavitis listened carefully, and became troubled at the mention of shooting.

'Was that necessary?' he asked.

'Mr Pezas can witness that he was being attacked. Viciously. I warned the redhead to stop. More than once. When he ignored me I opened fire.'

'Did they understand your warning?'

'I have no idea. Things were moving too fast. I had to save my friend's life.'

'Do you have a licence for a gun?'

'Licence and training.'

Kassavitis told his assistant to collect the men's possessions. George thought of the phone in his pocket, and made a quick decision to hold on to it.

Kassavitis asked the men something in Russian. They recognised the language. A short conversation followed.

Kassavitis turned to George. 'They say they were bringing you a message.'

'With crash-helmets and weapons? Nice message!'

'They don't know why you shot them.'

'They know damn nicely!'

'They say they don't.'

'Ask them why they attacked my friend. And why this one pulled a knife on me.'

Kassavitis asked, then translated the reply. 'Your friend attacked them first.'

'They're lying,' said George.

The officer had another short conversation in Russian.

'OK,' he said finally. 'I can see what we're dealing with.'

'I need to know who sent these men,' said George. 'And what they want from me.'

'I'll try to find out,' said Kassavitis.

The ambulance arrived, and they moved out.

24

The next morning at eight, he had a call from the young lieutenant, asking him to present himself at Exarchia police station by midday.

He finished his interrupted breakfast, picked up his passport and phone, and walked the four hundred metres to Kallidromiou Street. He was conscious, as he approached the station, that this was the centre of trouble eighteen months ago when a policeman had shot a teenager during a demonstration. That in turn had set off a chain reaction of riots, looting, vandalism and arson. The streets had calmed down since then, but the underlying anger still burned.

Kassavitis sat at his regulation doll's house desk with its regulation chaos of papers. He was tired and grim-faced.

'What's up? said George.

'I have to arrest you.'

'What for?'

'Assault.'

'On those bikers?'

'Their lawyer is pressing charges.'

'Their lawyer?'

'They insisted on calling him. We've been up half the night.'

'You heard what my colleague Mr Pezas said? They would have killed him!'

'It's their word against yours.'

'How about exercising a little common sense?'

'What do you mean by that?'

'Let's think about it. Two armed Russians call on you at eleven p.m...'

'And you shoot them.'

'They're about to do some serious damage to your friend's skull. They have a stick the size of a baseball bat, a pistol and two knives, and they start using them.'

'That's your story.'

'And my colleague's!'

'Two against two. I have to give equal weight to both sides.'

'Two criminals against two decent citizens?'

'They are not at this point known to be criminals.'

'So what are they? Jehovah's Witnesses?'

'I have to do this by the book. I have no choice.'

'They don't even speak Greek! What are they? Russians?'

'Georgians.'

'Even worse!'

'I must ask you to make a statement.'

'I'm happy to do that.'

'You have the right to call a lawyer.'

'No need. I have nothing to hide.'

'Right, let's go to the interview room and start.'

In a locked, bare-walled room without windows, George made his statement. The lieutenant, sitting on the opposite side of a wooden desk, took it down, word by word, with a cassette recorder running. At one point he asked if George had taken a phone belonging to one of the men. George said he had not. The text was read back to him and he signed it. He undertook not to leave the country and surrendered his passport by way of guarantee. The lieutenant was unable to tell him when he would have it back.

George asked about the two bikers.

'I'm not required to give you any information about them,' said Kassavitis. He switched off the tape recorder. 'They've been detained for unauthorised possession of firearms.'

'Firearms?' said George, surprised. 'Plural?'

'The redhead had a pistol in his boot.'

'Shit, I missed that. He could have used it.'

'The bullet in his shoulder made that unlikely,' said Kassavitis.

George nodded. 'How long will you hold them?'

'It depends what comes up when we check the records.'

'Can I press charges against them?'

'I don't see why not. But it might be more effective if Mr Pezas were to do it.'

'Good idea,' said George, 'I'll tell him to get onto it.'

The lieutenant ejected the cassette and slipped it into an envelope with the signed statement.

'Do I have to stay?' asked George.

'No,' said the lieutenant. 'You're free to go. But I'm keeping your passport as a temporary measure. And if you happen to find the phone, please bring it in.'

Kassavitis unlocked the interview room door.

He was home by ten, and on the telephone to Pezas. He gave him the news and asked if he would go down to Exarchia police station and make a statement.

'With the greatest of pleasure,' said Pezas. 'Only I'm in Kefalari right now. I have to see some people about those deaths in the bank. I should be done by noon.'

'Don't leave it too late. I don't want those bikers on the loose again. That young police lieutenant was OK, but he may decide to let them go if there's nothing in the records. He's a little too respectful of procedures for my liking.'

'Do you want me to come down now?'

'What about your other appointments?'

'I'll change them. Deal with the urgent stuff first.'

'It would be a big help.'

'OK, leave it to me.'

25

George cast his eye over his desk. For some reason it depressed him. The whole room depressed him. He had a sudden, overwhelming feeling of paralysis. He was stuck midway through a case, unpaid and getting nowhere. The police were arresting the wrong people, their investigations were logjammed, their staff overworked, the system riddled with corruption and abuse, their custody of evidence slapdash, and the only consistently applied rule was that the innocent should suffer while the guilty received every encouragement.

His usual approach at times like this was to plunge into action of some kind – it scarcely mattered what. Motivation would follow. All he could think of doing now, however, was calling his wife to see how she and Nick were getting along. He picked up the phone, but it rang before he could dial.

'Good morning, George! Abbas calling! I have news from the colonel.'

'Good news, I hope?'

'He is prepared to pay you 250 euros a day.'

'I told him my price.'

'He wishes to point out that there's an economic squeeze on. His pension has dropped by thirty percent. He suggests you play your part in the national sacrifice, and take a cut of a mere eighteen percent.'

'Did he say all that?'

'Effectively, yes. Although I ran the numbers for him.'

'He must be having one of his better days.'

'I suspect the arrest has concentrated his mind.'

'All right, tell him I'll accept his offer. But I need some money up front.'

'How much?'

'A thousand.'

'I'm sure that will be fine.'

Abbas was about to ring off but George stopped him. 'Have you had any luck with the gun?' he asked.

'No progress. I haven't had a moment. But I've been thinking.'

'Any results?'

'Results would be the wrong word.'

'What would be the right word?'

Abbas laughed. 'I don't care to encapsulate such a complex process in a single word.'

'All right then, what have you been thinking?'

'I believe we must stop following single threads and try to see the figure in the carpet.'

'Sorry, which carpet is this?'

'I'm speaking metaphorically. It's an image from Henry James.'

'Is that Henry James the jazz trumpeter?'

'No, Henry James the novelist and critic.'

'Listen, Abbas, I'm having a hard day. Suppose we talk in something other than riddles?'

'I'm thinking in terms of the pattern in the story. The deeper plot.'

'I'm still not with you. I studied economics. Not literature.'

'Economists talk of market cycles, correct?'

'They do.'

'That's an example of a pattern, observable only at a

distance and with special knowledge.'

'And over time.'

'Exactly.'

'Where is this leading?'

'I'm trying to see the deeper pattern in what's happening now.'

'Have you considered that it might just be chaos?'

'Superficially it's chaos,' said Abbas.

'It could be chaos all the way down,' said George. 'The colonel's under arrest, the evidence has been tampered with, the police are lost in the jungle of their own bureaucracy, and no one can see a way out.'

'You need to make sense of all that. Find the figure! You know what I would do? Meditate on the whole thing. Draw a diagram. Think about it. Let images come to mind. From your unconscious. Use parts of your brain that sense the wider reality.'

'You're confusing me again, Abbas. Am I supposed to think about this logically or intuitively?'

'Both!'

'Both at once?'

'If you can!'

'And how the hell do I do that?'

'First one, then the other. Toss it from hand to hand. Logic, intuition. Back and forth. Maybe I'll do the same. We'll compare our findings.'

George put down the phone, thinking Abbas had gone mad.

All the same, after a little thought, he decided to try it. From the drawer in his desk he took a blank sheet of paper. Without thinking too much, he drew four small circles at the points of the compass. In three he wrote the names of people who had died:

John Petrakis, Angelos Boiatzis, his wife's niece Anastasia. In the fourth, after a moment's superstitious hesitation, he wrote his own name. He didn't care to be numbered among the dead, but he reminded himself that this was only a sketch, an experiment in thought. Every circle was a victim, or intended victim.

Next to each he added one or more triangles, representing aggressors. 'Unknown anarchist' next to Anastasia, 'HK G3' next to John Petrakis, 'Russian bikers' next to himself. He contemplated the result. There were important parts of the story missing. He made another circle next to himself for Pezas, and a sixth circle near Petrakis for Colonel Varzalis. Next to the colonel he drew two sharp triangles, which he labelled 'Constantine Petrakis' and 'Simeon Yerakas'. This action put him in mind of another aggressor to add next to his own circle, 'Byron Kakridis'.

A minute spent staring at the page made him think of a third set of players: the police. They needed a new shape. He drew a square next to John Petrakis. That was Captain Bagatzounis. Next to himself he added Lieutenant Kassavitis. Above him, in the centre of the diagram, he drew a square with the name 'SOTIRIOU' in capitals.

The central placing of this last figure was accidental, yet oddly significant. Where else could he be located? All violent crimes were reported to Sotiriou's department, the investigations were started and managed there. Perhaps everything stalled there too? He had a vision of the ghastly office with its labyrinth of paper stacked in yellowing columns, a place of suffocation, entropy, and accumulating dust. Stuff was always moving into there. How did it ever move out?

Sotiriou liked to protest his probity. This alone made George uncomfortable. Most people who do that, he reflected, are sharks. Decency needs no advertising. Was it possible that Sotiriou was deliberately obstructing him? As corrupt as the worst of his colleagues, with the added vices of sanctimony, hypocrisy, and, most dangerous of all, self-delusion?

He walked over to the window. The sky was clear and blue between the buildings. The canary trilled from Dimitri's balcony while the traffic grumbled and hooted below. He tried to let his mind run free, out of this huge lattice of concrete, glass and steel, into the open spaces of the sky. He consciously blanked out all thought – just concentrated on that distant immensity of blue. A series of images came to him, detached from all words and entanglements of causation. They appeared, stayed a few moments, then vanished like slides on a screen. The hand-grip on the biker's pistol. The framed, silhouetted head. Colonel Varzalis firing his Hämmerli at that distant balloon. The empty hotel by the sea.

Were the images connected? Did they appear to him for a reason? Was this what Abbas meant by meditation?

The telephone started to ring. He picked it up and heard the voice of Pezas.

'Have you heard about the fire at Paranoia FM?'

'No, when?'

'Last night. I just heard the news on the radio.'

'Is anyone hurt?'

'No. They all escaped. But the station's ruined.'

'I'll check it out.'

George searched for Paranoia FM on the internet. He found the station's website, with a brief announcement of the news and a promise to be back on air within 48 hours. The address, he noticed, was Leoforos Alexandras – a fifteen minute walk. He decided to take a look.

26

A tall, bearded man with a bald head was standing in front of
a small neoclassical house with tongues of soot above empty
windows and doors. He was talking very fast and angrily to
a dapper executive in a pressed white shirt who was calmly
making notes on a clipboard. The roof was a skeleton of charred
timbers. A smell of burning – rubbery, acrid, repulsively
chemical – hung in the street.

George waited until the conversation was over. The dapper
man picked his way carefully into the building, stepping under
a band of security tape as he went. The bearded man began
punching text into his phone.

George approached him. 'Mr Ghiotis?'

'Who are you?'

'My name is George Zafiris. I'm a private detective.'

'No thanks.'

'I'm not looking for work.'

'What do you want?'

'I've been investigating the death of Angelos Boiatzis, the
MP. I gather you've been working on the same case.'

'So?'

'I wondered if we might talk.'

'No.'

'You don't know what I have to offer.'

'I don't have time now.'

'Because of the fire?'

'Yes, because of the fire!'

'I heard the news. I'm sorry.'

Ghiotis ignored him.

'When can I come back?' asked George.

'When the nightmare's over.'

Ghiotis returned to his phone.

'This is only going to get worse,' said George. 'Now's the time to act, before someone gets killed.'

Ghiotis gave him a cynical look.

'Killed?'

'It could easily have happened last night. Was there no one in the building?'

'That's none of your business.'

'Think it was an accident?'

'No way! This was arson.'

'Right. And who's responsible?'

'You think I know that?'

Ghiotis began text-messaging again.

George watched him for a few moments.

'Did you look into his love life?' asked George.

'What?' Ghiotis looked up abstractedly.

'Boiatzis had a mistress. His wife had a lover too.'

'Big deal.'

'Had any visits from Russian hit men recently?'

'No.'

'You will soon.'

'I'm ready for them.'

'Really? You have a bodyguard? Carry a gun? You look pretty vulnerable to me.'

Ghiotis stared at him blankly.

George took a card from his pocket. 'Call me if you want to talk,' he said.

Ghiotis glanced at the card, slid it into his pocket, then followed the other man into the burnt-out building.

27

The visitors' room at the prison was drab and hot, with hard wooden chairs and tables. Sunlight slanted in through high windows. Traffic was audible from outside. A warder sat watching suspiciously as Abbas took a ragged old folder of documents out of his briefcase and opened it on the table in front of him.

'This was all I could find,' he said.

'That's the one,' said the colonel. 'In there you should find a list of volunteers.'

'I've seen that,' said George. 'What I really want is a list of the weapons they possessed.'

'I have that too.'

'Really?' George glanced at Abbas. 'Can I see it?'

'Of course. It's in here somewhere.'

The colonel began leafing through the papers. Some he discarded at once. Others caught his attention. He began reading carefully, following the text with his finger. Abbas and George watched him with growing unease.

'Why don't I look through them for you?' said Abbas. 'It might be quicker.'

'It will definitely be quicker!' said the colonel.

He shoved the file across the table. 'All this paperwork! And what's it for? The flames!'

'I'm glad you haven't burnt them yet,' said George.

'It won't be long now,' said the colonel.

Abbas handed him a flimsy sheet of copy paper.

'Is this it?'

The colonel took it from him and read it.

'That,' he said, 'is a list of the volunteers and the weapons they owned.'

'You seem to have recruited the best of the ancient Greeks,' said Abbas. 'You have Alcibiades, Leonidas, Themistocles, Xenophon…'

'Not a bad squad! They're all codenames of course.'

'What was the purpose of that?' asked George.

The colonel looked mystified. 'Who knows?'

'Do you have a key? To decode them?' asked Abbas.

'I have no idea.'

'I'll keep looking.'

'You won't find it there,' said the colonel. 'Never keep the key near the code.'

'Let me look just the same,' said Abbas.

He went on through the papers, quickly, expertly. He set one sheet aside, and was soon at the end of the file. He turned the file over, checked it was empty, ran a hand around the inside.

'No key in there,' he said. 'You've left us with a puzzle.'

The colonel looked pleased.

'Why the secrecy?' said Abbas.

'Secrecy is strength!' The colonel smiled.

'You military guys can't ever call a spade a spade. Either it's got some damn stupid code number like "P22" or you dress it in absurd technical jargon like "manually deployed excavation facilitator".'

'There's a good reason for that,' said the colonel.

'Really? I'd like to know what it is. Because anyone looking through your files would be able to find out at once who your volunteers are…'

'No!'

'Oh yes! Their names and addresses are listed.'

'They shouldn't be.'

Jalal showed him the piece of paper he had set aside. 'Here they are.'

'That list must be destroyed!'

'No! That list is precious. But the strange thing is that one list is coded, the other not.'

'The coded one is the right one,' said the colonel.

'But we can't crack the code!'

'You can compare the two lists.'

'There's no cross-reference. Look, here's the gun we want, the Heckler & Koch G3. That belonged to "Xenophon". But who in hell is "Xenophon"?'

'Let me see,' said the colonel.

Abbas handed him the two sheets. He studied them for a while, focussed at first, then increasingly puzzled. His eyes became vague.

'I don't understand a word of it,' he said.

'Can you remember anyone on that list?'

'I think I'm Socrates.'

'You've no idea who Xenophon might be?'

The colonel seemed distressed. His mouth was shut tight, his eyes shifty.

'It's OK,' said Abbas. 'We'll leave it.'

George had an idea. 'We can ask the three that we know already. They can tell us their codenames.'

'If they know them,' said Abbas.

'Why do you say that?'

'Looking at this list, I must be Aeschylus, because Aeschylus has a Colt pistol and a Remington rifle. Those are my weapons. But I didn't know my codename. I didn't even know I had a codename!'

'Ah…'

'We'll do some cross-referencing,' said Abbas. 'Narrow it down.' He glanced at the warder, who was showing signs of interest in their conversation. 'I think we should leave the colonel now.'

At a café nearby Abbas and George examined the two lists.

The first was new to George. It gave codenames and some weapon details, but no names or addresses.

Aeschylus	* Remington
	+ Colt
Ajax	* Sako
Alcibiades	+ Heckler & Koch P30
Hector	x Beretta 687
Daedalus	* Winchester 70
Leonidas	* Mauser 98K
Pericles	* Fabarm
Nestor	* Mauser 98K
	+ CZ 75B
Odysseus	* Mauser 98K
Xenophon	* Heckler & Koch G3
Phidias	* Weihrauch
Philoctetes	* Daystate
Miltiades	* Miroku
Themistocles	x Sarasqueta
Socrates	* Lee Enfield, Hämmerli
	+ Browning Hi-Power, Glock 19
	x Purdey, Fabbri, AYA

The second list gave names and addresses, with a generic weapon code:

*	Pangalos, Harilaos	Dimokratias 23, Marathonas
*	Maginas, Andonis	Venizelou 10, Souvala
*	Tsaousoglou, Aris	Lazarides
*	Paraskevás, Ioannis	Irioti 5, Aegina
*	Kotsis, Leonardos	Vyzantiou 1, Aegina
*+	Kalamaras, Andreas	Aristotelous 6, Aegina
x	Philippidis, Iason	Aghias Irinis 7, Aegina
*+	Tsoublekas, Manolis	Aghiou Nikolaou 33, Aegina
*+	Abbas, Jalal	Mitropoleos 6, Aegina
*	Tasakos, Manos	Psaron 4, Aegina
*	Laskaradis, Stephanos	Apheas 123, Aegina
x	Hitiris, Spyridon	Perdika
*+x	Varzalis, Solon	Telamonos 18, Aegina
x	Doukakis, Theodoros	Aghia Marina
+	Gounaris, Mihalis	Trikoupi 15, Souvala

'We have three of the fifteen right away,' said George. 'Aeschylus is you, Socrates is the colonel, Leonidas is the policeman…'

'And Daedalus is the pilot.'

'How do we know that?'

'He has a Winchester.'

'Daedalus was also the first airman,' said George. 'I wonder if the codes are connected to people's jobs?'

'Possibly. I'm an author, though not quite up there with Aeschylus.'

'Ancient Leonidas wasn't a policeman.'

'No, but he was a Spartan, and Kotsis is a Spartan too.'

'OK, so how about the colonel as Socrates?' said George. 'What's the link?'

'I don't see one,' said Abbas. 'The names are random.'

'So who else do you know here?'

Abbas read through the list again.

'We could eliminate six more. Some of these people live out of town. Others have pistols or shotguns, not rifles.'

'That doesn't necessarily mean anything. They could have bought new weapons, or come into town specially.'

'Drive into town, park the car, take out a rifle and hang about in the back streets waiting for Professor Petrakis to take a shower? Hoping no one sees you?'

'OK, it sounds bloody stupid. So we eliminate the out-of-towners.'

Abbas went down the list. 'Pangalos, Maginas, Tsaousoglou, Hitiris, Gounaris, Doukakis.'

'That leaves four names: Kalamaras, Tsoublekas, Tasakos, Laskaridis. What do we know about them?'

'Kalamaras has an electrical shop. Tsoublekas is a lawyer.

Tasakos we've met. He doesn't have his gun any more and he was in Athens that day. Laskaridis is an architect.'

'Do any of these four belong to extreme patriotic organisations?'

'How do I know? Not Laskaridis anyway. He's a liberal.'

'A liberal and a gun-owner?'

'It happens.'

'Really?'

'Look at me. Shooting gets into your blood. You do it for fun once or twice, and before you know it you're a member of the Rifle Club.'

'In my view,' said George, 'there's something inherently authoritarian in using a gun.'

'On other living creatures, yes. On a target, no. The authority isn't you, it's the goddess Accuracy.'

'Is Laskaridis a suspect?'

'I would eliminate him on grounds of character, but perhaps that's unscientific.'

'What about the other three?'

'Your guess is as good as mine.'

'So we need to see Kalamaras and Tsoublekas. Find out if they had anything against the professor.'

'Correct. If I might make a suggestion?'

'What's that?'

'You should go at this indirectly. I've watched you asking questions. You're far too direct! They know at once what you're after. That gives them time to prepare a lie.'

'How would you approach them?'

'Why not say you want to buy a gun?'

'You think they'd fall for that?'

'They might.'

'But I've already been going round talking to people about

the murder. I can't just change my story.'

'No one will notice.'

'I don't like deceiving people.'

'If I had the murder weapon in my house and you came round asking questions about the professor, I would have no hesitation in deceiving you. I certainly wouldn't tell you anything useful.'

'Not consciously. But your unconscious signals might. Guilty people try to close down the inquiry. They'll often do something odd. The innocent have nothing to hide.'

Abbas thought about this.

'You know what?' he said. 'I have another idea. Why don't I talk to these guys myself? After all, I know them. I could say I'm writing a history of the volunteer force. Trying to find out the codenames.'

'I like that better.'

'I could even see the out-of-towners, on the off-chance they might know who owns the G3.'

'Brilliant.'

'The code may turn out to be our friend.'

*

On the ferry back to Athens, George thought again about the shooting of the professor. The angle of entry in the forensic report had been 25 degrees left of the mid-line, 15 below. The colonel's garden fitted the profile perfectly. The internet man's house was on the right of the mid-line, as was the policeman's. Only the pilot, Daedalus, was as well placed as the colonel for the shooting. Yet neither of these could seriously be accused of the murder. Whoever did it might equally have shot from the back streets, or even from the colonel's garden…

Yet there was something else to consider. These angles of entry, vertical and lateral, must depend on the orientation of the professor's head at the moment of impact. If he was facing the window, a bullet fired from the colonel's house would have hit the left side of his head. If he was facing away from the window, to the left, the same bullet would have hit the right side of his head. In other words the bullet could have come from left or right. A similar uncertainty obtained as to the vertical angle. If his head was upright, a shot fired from an upstairs window would strike it horizontally. But suppose the head was tilted back – say he was rinsing his hair – then the same shot would enter from below, or appear to. Thus the angles of entry might be misleading. The shot could have come from either side, above or below; an upstairs window, a roof, a balcony, even the street.

Frustrated, George tried to think of other things. Forcing his mind away from the obsessive microscopic mapping of that single destructive moment, he turned his gaze to the present – the fluid, slippery present, always moving, never to be seized – and the dazzling arena of sea and sky through which the *Aghios Nektarios* was gliding like a ghost. It was a familiar scene, yet it began changing before his eyes, flaring out into a photographic negative of itself, where white stood for black and black for white. The mountains dissolved into air, the sea into smoke, the sky hardened into sheet metal. The furious heat transformed everything, vaporising rock and condensing light and air into hard-edged solids. Even with the sea breeze blowing, the sun felt like a surgeon's blade cutting through him. He felt light-headed, transparent, as if every atom in his body had turned to pure oxygen.

It lasted fifteen seconds, no more. Then the heat seeped into him, began cooking his brain. It was time to move.

He walked along the deck to the heavy steel door that led into the bar. As he swung it open, a blast of cold air engulfed him. He ordered an iced coffee, still in a near-hallucinatory state, hearing his voice as if it belonged to someone else. He found a seat at a small table, sipped his coffee and made an attempt to gather himself.

A television was gabbling in a corner of the saloon. A woman with swollen legs propped on a chair was eating a cake and staring at her thin, worried husband with a look of hatred. A mother sat contentedly with her two small children, one on either side of her, curled up and fast asleep.

With his head cooling down, George pursued an idea that had begun to form in the heat outside. It was to do with negatives and silhouettes, cut-outs and the shapes that are left behind.

He took out his phone and called Takis Mitropoulos.

'Taki, can you do me a favour? I need a photocopy of the Aegina firearms register. Every page. Can you organise that?'

'I'm not sure, George.'

'What's the problem?'

'They're keeping the documents locked away for the special investigator. I broke the rules when I looked at the forensic report. I've been up before a superior for that.'

'How come?'

'I asked to see the documents and someone reported me. The papers are hot. It's not my case and I had to explain my interest in it. That was tricky.'

'Why?'

'The simplest explanation fills them with suspicion. "Helping a friend" translates into "I'm a member of a criminal network". If you're genuine they go crazy because they can't spot the trick.'

'All I'm trying to do is keep an innocent man out of prison! And put a guilty one in. The police would be doing it if they weren't such slaves to their bloody procedures!'

'I know that, George.'

'Is there nothing you can do?'

Takis was silent for a few moments.

'Let me give it some thought,' he said finally. 'My story has to stand up.'

'It has to be consistent with the first one, presumably.'

'OK. So why am I going back?'

'Different document.'

'I can't photocopy it, George. They'll kill me.'

'Photograph it?'

'No. The most I can do is consult it. In front of an officer.'

'Could you check it against a list of names?'

'How long is the list?'

'Fifteen names.'

'Fifteen? That's quite a few... And one of them is the killer?'

'Very probably.'

'Only he won't be in the register, because the page has been removed?'

'Exactly. The missing one is the prime suspect.'

'Suppose there's more than one name missing?'

'It's still better than fifteen.'

Takis took a few moments to think about this.

'All right,' he said at last. 'I'll try. Where's the list?'

'I'll email it to you when I get home. A couple of hours from now.'

'I can't guarantee anything, George.'

'That's understood.'

For the next part of the journey home – entering the harbour at Piraeus, tying up, leaving the ship and dodging along the filthy pavements, through the crowd of trinket-sellers to the railway station – George fought a battle inside himself between anger and detachment. Anger was justified but useless. Detachment was necessary but unattainable. The two impulses slugged it out, too evenly matched to produce a quick result. Once he was on the train, rattling uptown towards Omonia, the tussle died down. He took a notebook and pen from his pocket and made a list of the things the police ought to be doing and probably weren't. As soon as he arrived home he would send the email to Takis, then get on the phone to Sotiriou. Better still he would go and see him. Eyeball the man, show him some righteous rage.

28

'I can give you five minutes,' said Sotiriou.

'That's all I need. Can we go up to your office?'

'Not now.'

They were standing in the entrance lobby of the Violent Crimes Building, a bare, grim space with nowhere to sit down. The only furniture was a desk and chair occupied by a bored young policeman.

OK, thought George, have it your way.

In a deliberately neutral voice he said, 'I need to ask you some questions.'

Sotiriou said nothing. His eyes rested calmly on George. Waiting.

'Question one: have you spoken to Sophocles Ghiotis about the fire at Paranoia FM?'

Sotiriou was silent.

'Question two: have you checked the pistols carried by the Russian bikers who attacked my colleague the other night? Question three: have you investigated the abuse of the Aegina firearms register?'

Sotiriou watched him as he spoke, his eyes two slits reflecting the grey light of the lobby.

'Well?' said George.

'All of these matters are being investigated.'

'Meanwhile two innocent people are arrested.'

'Two?'

'Colonel Varzalis and myself.'

'I have just signed the papers for Colonel Varzalis to be released on grounds of ill health. Pending trial, that is. It will be months, if not years, before his case comes before a judge. Or yours for that matter. Meanwhile you're free to operate, travel, work…'

'I am not free to travel! My passport is being held.'

'I meant in Greece.'

'Suppose I need to go abroad?'

Sotiriou shrugged. 'I'm sure something can be arranged.'

George felt like picking him up by the collar and smashing him into the wall. 'When we first met,' he said, 'you told me you were against corruption. You gave me a great speech about discipline and order. I believed you. Now I think you're lying like the rest of them. Worst of all, you're lying to yourself. The system's rotten right through! If you create a little area of discipline and order, all you do you is slow things down!'

'OK, I've heard what you've got to say, so now…'

'There'll be more deaths soon. You'll see.'

'What are you talking about?'

'Ghiotis, Varzalis, maybe me.'

'Just be patient. It will all work out.'

'If you do nothing else,' said George, 'check those Russian bikers' guns against forensic and ballistic reports. I'll put money on their involvement…'

'It will be done.'

'When? That's the question!'

'I have to go.'

Sotiriou turned towards the lift and pressed the call button. The lift doors opened. He was about to move forward, but stopped. Standing inside the lift was Kakridis, explosive with rage. His two bodyguards, sensing the tension, reached into their jackets.

'Minister –' Sotiriou began.

Kakridis cut him off impatiently. 'Forget it,' he said, and hurried out.

Sotiriou seemed confused. He stood paralysed for a moment, torn between pursuing Kakridis and letting him go. Then he stepped into the lift and was gone.

As he walked home, George considered what he had seen. It was a fair bet that Kakridis had been in Sotiriou's office. The meeting did not seem to have gone well. And why was the minister visiting the policeman, not the policeman the minister? This was odd.

His thoughts were interrupted by a call from Pezas.

'I'm with Mrs Kakridis,' he said. 'She wants to talk to us both. Urgently. In a private place.'

'Where are you?'

'Kolonaki.'

'Can you come to my flat? I'll be there in twenty minutes.'

He hurried on. The phone rang again. It was Takis.

'I tried to see the firearms register but it's not here anymore.'

'You're joking!'

'It's vanished.'

'Some official must have taken it.'

'There's no evidence of that. The special investigator's mystified. My only guess is that it got into the wrong removal box.'

'What a bloody circus!'

'By the way, I know one of the names on the list.'

'Which one?'

'Leonardos Kotsis. The retired policeman.'

'And?'

'Nothing wrong with him. He's a good man.'

'I had that impression.'

'I'm glad about that. Stay in touch.'

*

Mrs Kakridis sat in the armchair by the French window, a stylish figure in a cream linen dress. Her bare, tanned legs were crossed. Her nicely cut dark hair framed a troubled face. George found it hard at first not to think of the photographs he had taken of her at her husband's request, at the window of a hotel room. Then she started to say things that made him forget the past.

'My husband's not a bad man,' she said. 'He believes in his party, believes in Greece. He's been good to me and the children.'

'That sounds like the prelude to bad news,' said George.

She glanced at him darkly. 'There's been a change.'

'What sort of change?'

'His manner… His attitude to me.'

'Are we talking about the affair with Mrs Boiatzis?'

'No. Apart from that. Something deeper. His character has hardened. He's lost the kindness he once had.'

'What do you expect us to do about that?' said Pezas. 'We're detectives, not marriage counsellors.'

'He's also keeping bad company.'

'What do you mean?'

'Men who drive around in jeeps with tinted windows. Mean-faced. Their chauffeurs look military. Lots of muscle. They have the paranoid look of professional security men. Only these guys are on the wrong side. They're the people you hire security to protect you against.'

'How can you be sure they're "on the wrong side", as you put it?'

'There's an atmosphere about them. Good people don't give me the creeps like that.'

'Anything else?'

'They come to the house at strange times.'

'Have you talked to them?'

'Never. My husband deals with them. They talk outside the house.'

'Long conversations?'

'Five, ten minutes.'

'Does money change hands?'

'I don't know.'

'Have you taken any photos of these people? Or noted down the number plates of their cars?'

'No.'

'It would help if you could do that.'

She gave George a challenging look.

'Isn't that your speciality?'

He wondered if her husband had shown her the photographs of her infidelity.

'All forms of surveillance are our speciality,' he said. 'But if we do it, it's going to cost. Not just for the pictures but the waiting time. On the other hand if you do it...'

'The cost is no problem.'

'There are logistical difficulties too. We would need to install video cameras without your husband's knowledge.'

'Suppose you just waited outside the house? When they come I'll alert you.'

'24-hour live surveillance? That's extremely expensive.'

'I've told you, the cost is irrelevant.'

'Are there plenty of cars parked in your street?' asked

Pezas.

'A few. Why?'

'We don't want to be noticed. How about security firms patrolling the area?'

'Several.'

'Then the street's too risky. They'll be onto us quick as anything.'

'I have another idea,' said George. 'Can you borrow your husband's phone for an hour?'

'Possibly at night, when he's asleep. Why?'

'I want a list of the numbers he's called in the last two weeks.'

'He's very touchy about his phone.'

'Of course…'

'But then he's touchy about a lot of things.'

'What about his computer?'

'Out of bounds!'

'Why's that?'

'He says women don't understand technology.'

'Predictable. His desk?'

'He doesn't like me to touch anything.'

'Can you take a discreet look?'

'He'd notice.'

'When he's away from home?'

'He locks everything. He's incredibly precise and methodical. I'd need to copy his keys, sneak in there when the staff aren't looking, and leave everything exactly as I found it. To the nearest millimetre.'

'It can be done if you're careful.'

'I don't trust myself.'

'Does he have security cameras? Alarms?'

'The full package.'

'What do you think your husband's up to?' asked Pezas.

'I wish I knew!'

'This is all so vague…'

'I understand that. But a wife knows when her husband changes.'

'What do you hope to achieve by getting us involved?'

'If he's doing something illegal, I want to stop him.'

'How will you stop him?'

'I'll confront him.'

'Will that be enough?'

'It always has been in the past. I don't think he'll risk losing me.'

'Is there a special reason for that?' asked Pezas.

'You don't need to know. Just take my word for it.'

'OK,' said George, 'I think we can make a start. Find a time to borrow your husband's phone. It may cost you a sleepless night.'

'That's OK.'

They agreed terms and Mrs Kakridis left.

'Unhappy woman,' said Pezas.

'Wouldn't you be, married to that man?'

'What do you think he's up to?'

'I don't know. I bumped into him today at the Violent Crimes Unit. My guess is he's trying to frighten Sotiriou.'

'Was Sotiriou helpful?'

'To Kakridis or me?'

'You.'

'No. I don't know whose side he's on. I'm not even sure he does.'

Pezas sat thinking in silence.

'Somewhere this must all crack open,' he said.

Feeling suddenly thirsty, George suggested, 'Beer?'

'Sounds good to me.'

He brought two cold Amstels from the fridge and levered off the caps.

'I see two ways to go forward,' said Pezas. 'One through Mrs Kakridis. The other through your radio man, Ghiotis.'

'He's no help.'

'True, but he's stirring things up. Maybe we can give him a lead or two?'

'I've tried that. He's made of the same hard stuff as Sotiriou. Knows it all. Won't listen.'

'Let's see what his website says. That might give us an opening.'

George opened his laptop and brought up Paranoia FM. A bland corporate website appeared, with studio shots of the presenters and too many advertising links.

'This is bullshit,' said George.

'I think Ghiotis has a blog,' said Pezas. 'Try that.'

George quickly found it: a crude, urgent page, without a hint of commerce. They scrolled through some recent entries.

Greece's enslavement to the IMF continues… New humiliations… What happened to our rights? Pensioners betrayed… The slow death of a railway network… Whose environment? Democracy for sale… Is your workplace a death trap?

'Hold on,' said George. 'Let's look at that.'

They clicked on the 'workplace' link and found a short article about the fire in the bank in May. 'People who throw molotov cocktails into banks are idiots – we all know that. What turned them into killers was the bank's indifference to the lives of their staff. By locking the fire exits, the bank turned a political gesture into a murder. The police should prosecute the executives of the bank. They are the real killers.'

'Is that right?' asked George. 'About the fire exits?'

'I haven't checked.'

'The bank could be liable for compensation.'

'Even if he's right, I don't like his tone.'

'Why not?'

'It's nasty, snide, accusing.'

'Understandably!'

Pezas was getting animated. 'He's a communist. Usual crap. Banks, capitalism, government. Plenty of criticism. No constructive programme.'

'Usable fire exits seems like a pretty constructive programme to me.'

'Look at the rest of it. He's supporting all these strikes, attacking the EU and the IMF, he's totally irresponsible!'

'Let's see what he says about defence contracts...'

He clicked on *Banquet of the Death Merchants*.

'Typical cheap shot,' said Pezas. 'These bastards never stop to think what would happen to our country if we didn't have properly equipped armed forces! Or what would happen to their precious freedom of speech!'

'He doesn't seem to be against proper equipment. He's against officials taking bribes. Look! "Members of the past and present governments are named in a secret report into corruption and 'sweeteners' over the supply of German submarines to the Greek navy at grossly inflated prices. Investigations continue into purchase deals for other big-budget items: tanks, helicopters, armoured cars, fighter aircraft and radar systems. While we tighten our belts, the statesmen who rule us are stuffing their foreign bank accounts with black money." You think that's all right, do you?'

'No of course I don't! But who are these people? He names

no one.'

'OK, here it is. "Who's responsible? Over the next few weeks, Paranoia FM will tell the full story. Be ready to tune in to Sophocles Ghiotis on Sunday evening." '

'There you are! He's self-righteous about other people earning money, but he's perfectly happy to earn it himself.'

'He's got to live.'

'Bah! He disgusts me. We'll never have a mature democracy while political debate stays at that infantile level.'

'Next you'll be saying "bring back the colonels".'

'I do say that! At least they did what a government is supposed to do. Ensure law and order. Build roads. Defend us against enemies at home and abroad.'

George yawned. He had never suspected Pezas of being so ferociously right-wing.

29

The next day the breeze died and an Athenian heatwave began. Leaves hung limply from the trees, dry and papery. Air was in short supply. Cars and buses sloshed along the streets on melting tyres through clouds of black exhaust. When the temperature hit 40 degrees, people started talking about *káfsonas* – a state of burning.

George loathed this heat. Everything seemed stuck, drained of energy – out in the city and inside his head. His investigations were getting nowhere. It was the end of the week, the end of his patience.

He picked up the phone and called Zoe.

'How's it going?' she asked.

'Absolutely fucking awful,' he said. 'I need a break.'

'Come to Andros!'

'What are you up to?' he asked.

'Swimming twice a day, meals on the terrace with Nick. Peaches on the tree.'

'I'm coming.'

He packed a bag and looked up the times of the ferries. He tidied his desk and checked his watch. It was just before noon. An hour to drive to Rafina, then onto the ship at one thirty. And bugger everything else.

As he picked up his car keys, the telephone rang.

'Mr Zafiris? This is Colonel Sotiriou.'

'What can I do for you?'

'We followed your suggestion about the guns your visitors were carrying.'

'And?'

'Makarov pistols, Soviet army issue, 9 millimetre.'

'Illegally imported?'

'Correct.'

George wondered where this was leading.

'I'm calling you,' said Sotiriou, 'totally off the record. This conversation is not taking place.'

'I understand.'

'One of those pistols fired the bullet that killed Boiatzis.'

George felt his chest tighten.

'You're sure about that?'

'We are.'

'It makes suicide look unlikely,' said George.

'That's putting it mildly.'

'So you're detaining them?'

'Of course. They'll be questioned, and with luck we'll find out who sent them.'

'Thank you for keeping me informed. I was beginning to lose hope.'

'I must thank you, Zafiris. It was your suggestion. Made somewhat aggressively, I have to say, but when I thought it over I decided you were right.'

'Does this mean the charges against me will be dropped?'

'Which ones?'

'For so-called assault on the bikers.'

'That I can't tell you. But at least they won't be calling on you again.'

He was at the door when his phone rang again. He cursed.

'Hello, Mr Zafiris. This is Margarita Kakridis. I've done as you asked.'

'What exactly have you done?'

'I've made a list of calls from and to my husband's phone, and I have the registration number of a car.'

'That was very quick.'

'He had a visit last night. A short one, but it was enough. I got the phone numbers while he was sleeping. What shall I do with them?'

George hesitated. He wanted to get away.

'I'm on my way out of town,' he said. 'Can I come to you?'

'That's fine. Call when you get here. Don't ring the bell.'

He drove north along Leoforos Kifissias, past Halandri, Psychiko, Maroussi, the sun glaring viciously off windscreens and empty roadside showrooms – concrete and glass hangars with 'To Rent' notices stuck on their windows. After Syngrou Park he turned off, weaving through a labyrinth of narrow streets to the cemetery at Kefalari. He skirted the walls of the dark, cypress-filled plot, a silent reminder of death in this manic ant-hill of a city. He followed Trikoupi Street for a few hundred metres, then turned right. The Kakridis mansion stood well back from the road, behind high walls with security cameras. An enormous grey steel gate blocked the entrance, guarded by a man in a tiny glass cabin. George called Mrs Kakridis from his car.

After a minute the gate slid open. With a nod to the guard he drove through. At the end of the drive, among olive and fig trees, stood a vast plate-glass and concrete palace.

Margarita Kakridis was at the front door. She wore cream linen trousers, a pale green shirt, sleeves half-rolled, a gold necklace at her throat.

'Thank you for coming,' she said, the tension lines around

her mouth even more marked than yesterday.

She led him through a shady hallway, paved in slate and hung with expensive-looking art.

They walked out of the far side of the house, into the heat and glare. Past a 25-metre swimming pool with barbecue and changing rooms, to a circular terrace under an olive tree. Four grey metal chairs were arranged around a table. An immense view of Athens spread out below them. George took a seat, noticing only then that a Filippino manservant in a steward's uniform had followed them out.

'What will you have to drink?' asked Mrs Kakridis.

'Something cold, please.'

'Strawberry juice? I often have one at this time of day.'

'That sounds good.'

'Bring two, Simon,' she said.

'Yes, madam.'

Once Simon had vanished into the house she took a wad of folded notepaper from her back pocket and handed it quickly to George. He began to open it but she stopped him.

'Later,' she said.

He folded it away.

'Simon?' he said.

She nodded.

'How will you explain my visit?'

'You're a client of my gallery.'

'You have a gallery? I didn't know.'

'Why should you? When Simon comes back we'll talk about art.'

'In that case you'd better do the talking.'

'I'll keep it simple.'

'How many numbers have you given me?' asked George.

'I didn't count.'

'And the car?'

'Black Mercedes. The number's there too.'

'Any photos?'

'No. It was dark. Here come the drinks… I advise against Impressionists. They're overpriced now, even the minor ones. You'd be better going for early 20th century, including certain war artists. Is it landscapes you particularly like?'

He was not quite sure how to reply. Simon stood between them, pouring the bright red juice from a tall jug.

'I like portraits too,' said George. 'I'm interested in faces, in physiognomy.'

'Excellent. Nice contrast. Normally what I do in these circumstances is visit the house you're hoping to decorate, then put together a list of suitable works for each room.'

'That sounds good.'

'Anything else, madam?' asked Simon.

'No thank you. I'll call if we need anything.'

Simon made a little bow and returned slowly to the house.

She continued to talk art until he was out of earshot. Switching abruptly, she said, 'I'm very nervous.'

'Why?'

'I feel I'm betraying my husband.'

'You're not betraying him at all. You're trying to protect him.'

'But at what cost?'

'So far no cost at all, at least from my point of view.'

'I meant emotional cost.'

'That's a different matter,' said George. 'I have no way of helping you with that. But don't forget, he put you in this position.'

She nodded, anxious again. 'I was brought up to believe in a wife's duty to her husband.'

'You mean, the man is always right?'

She shrugged. 'Something like that.'

'It's rubbish,' said George. 'Old Greek macho bullshit. A formula for misery. Forget it. This is for his own good. For the family too.'

'So I try to tell myself.'

She sipped her drink. George watched her mask-like face, the slow, tense movement of the throat muscles as she swallowed.

'You seem to be afraid of your husband,' he said.

'Why do you say that?'

'A feeling, that's all.'

'It's probably true.'

'Is the telephone bugged?'

'I expect so.'

'Cameras in the rooms?'

She nodded.

'Out here?'

'There are cameras everywhere. My husband is very security-conscious.'

'He'll recognise me, won't he?'

'He won't watch the footage. Only if there's an incident.'

'Has he ever been violent?'

'No!'

She spoke too quickly.

'I'm not sure I believe you.'

She glared at him. 'Stick to your business, Mr Zafiris!'

'I'm sorry. I want to help, that's all.'

'You can find better ways!'

'All right.'

He drained his glass. 'That's good juice,' he commented. 'Tastes fresh.'

'It is fresh,' she said coldly.

He stood up. 'I'll go now. I have a ferry to catch. I'll check the papers this weekend. Please call me or Mr Pezas if you feel yourself to be in danger. At any time.'

'Thank you.'

On the road to Rafina he thought about her as he listened distractedly to the radio news. A woman in a miserable situation, struggling to keep up appearances, to keep her family safe, while her husband behaved like an idiot. Like thousands of others. All over the country. All over the world.

The newsreader babbled on about a strike by civil servants, protesting at cuts in their salaries and reductions in their numbers. They planned, a spokesman said, to paralyse the country. George felt no sympathy. Although many provided essential services, and were already poorly paid, a significant proportion were parasites and bureaucrats who did nothing for their fellow citizens but obstruct them with futile procedures and take bribes to circumvent them. They had paralysed the country for decades. He was reaching to turn off the radio when a newsflash came up.

George was suddenly focussed, listening intently. Sophocles Ghiotis had been shot. Two men dressed as security guards had called at his house early this morning and lured him into the street, claiming that someone was stealing his car. He had been found, badly injured and unconscious, by a neighbour walking his dog. He was now in intensive care, condition critical. Police were hoping he would recover consciousness and identify his attackers.

George considered driving back to Athens. But was there anything useful he could do? Ghiotis had refused to have dealings with him. If he recovered it would be days before he could talk to the police. It might never happen. Ghiotis might die, taking his revelations with him. Either way, there was nothing to be gained by going back. He drove on.

*

At the sight of the sea, George felt a release of tension in his heart. He parked the car and walked over to the ticket agencies, where girls in T-shirts and miniskirts were tempting customers in with strange mechanical cries: *Ya Androtinomykono! Androtinomykono!* 'Tickets to Andros, Tinos, Mykonos!'

He chose the plainest-looking girl, who welcomed him with a happy smile and led him to the counter, where her grim controller, a man in his fifties who had not shaved or changed his shirt for several days, issued a ticket while smoking a cigarette, never once meeting his eyes.

On board he bought an iced coffee and began reading through the telephone numbers, his diary open on the page for June 22nd, where he had written down the number of the Georgians' boss. Three hundred numbers to check. This could be a long job. On a computer it would take a couple of seconds, but this had to be done by hand.

He shut his mind to all else – the television blathering at a row of empty seats, the bar with its hissing coffee machines, the bleeping of the till, the safety announcements, the rambling banalities of people on mobile phones. He focussed on the last four numbers: 4605. He was soon asleep.

He woke up with the announcement on the ship's public address system that they were entering the harbour of Gavrio. Rapidly draining his coffee, now watery with melted ice cubes, he gathered up his things as the anchors rattled down and the ship juddered towards the jetty.

He drove south along the coast road. At Batsi he turned up into the hills, a lush valley leading to limestone country, the route twisting up a bare mountainside towards the sky. He came at last to the village of Arni: a scattering of houses and trees among the rocks. The air was cool and clear, the silence immense.

Zoe's house stood next to a spring on the far side of the village, a white cube among green foliage. The sight of it made him feel good.

At the sound of the car, Zoe came out of the house to meet him, in shorts and an old shirt splashed with fruit stains.

'At last,' she said, kissing him on the cheek.

'I can't tell you how glad I am to be here,' he said.

He gave no thought to work for twenty-four hours. He helped his wife peel, slice and cook the first peaches in sugar and water, then pour them hot into jars with their syrup. At eight they went out for a walk, high into the herb-scented crags. The sun's heat was fading, the fierce white light turning yellow, gold, then coppery-crimson as the day ripened and died. At nine they came home and found Nick on the verandah, sitting quietly with a can of cold beer.

He greeted his father and at once asked how long till supper. Zoe said it would be ready in half an hour.

'Great,' said Nick. 'I'm ravenous.'

He followed her into the kitchen, and came out a few moments later with a beer and a glass, which he placed in front of George. He asked how things were going in Athens.

George grimaced.

'Any more trouble?'

'A little. But it's fixed now.'

Nick looked relieved.

'I came here to clear my head,' said George.

'You're in the right place.'

George took a sip of beer.

'Stay as long as you can,' said Nick. 'We miss you.'

That night, after supper, with a pale half-moon hovering in the southern sky, Zoe and George sat out on the roof and drank wine, held by the silence of the mountains. They remembered happy times – their first meeting in London, holidays as students, their wedding, the early years with Nick.

'It makes me sad to think how all that's gone,' he said. 'I'd give anything to have it back.'

'It doesn't have to be gone.'

'No, but it is.'

'No, but it doesn't have to be.'

'What are you saying?'

'You know what I'm saying… We don't have to be strangers, George.'

'Really?'

She offered her hand. He took it.

30

The weekend was over too quickly. By eight on Monday morning he was down at Gavrio again, waiting for the ferry to come in. Gradually his mind adjusted, from dinner on the terrace and the candle-lit bedroom to the tangled web of lies, obstructions and suppositions that lay across his horizon like smog over Athens, a toxic cloud of uncertainty that he must enter and pass through. Could anything in that vast mess be 'solved'? Any questions be properly answered? Would he ever be able to say *There, that's dealt with*? It seemed a luxury beyond imagining.

In the ship's bar he ordered a filter coffee and sat down with Mrs Kakridis's list of phone numbers. He soon felt sleepy again, hypnotised by the lines of figures and the rhythmic throbbing of the engines. He shook himself awake, took a brisk walk around the deck, and returned to the task.

Suddenly he saw it: 4605. He checked with his diary. All ten numbers matched. On the list, this number appeared as 'Thanasis, Dentist', but that scarcely mattered. It was unlikely that Kakridis and the Georgian biker used the same dentist. They had business together. This was evidence.

For a moment George felt guilty. He should have done this two days ago. Then he stopped himself. Two days ago he had been a wreck. He wouldn't have done anything useful with the information. Now he was ready for action.

Back at his desk at noon, he rang Sotiriou.

'This is potentially a very serious allegation,' said the colonel. 'How many conversations did they have?'

'The number appears six times altogether.'

'Of course it's not proof.'

'No. Just run a check on the number, and on a black Mercedes, registration TMY 7582. You'll find out what kind of people Kakridis has been consorting with.'

'It could be perfectly innocent.'

'I don't see how.'

'He might have been trying to buy the man's car.'

'Late at night? I don't think so.'

'You realise we're talking about a government minister? With parliamentary immunity and the power to do some extremely nasty things to us?'

'I do. But so far he knows nothing of this. We have the advantage.'

'I'm not so sure,' said Sotiriou.

'You mean he knows he's being watched?'

Instead of answering, Sotiriou asked, 'Who's the source of information about the car and the telephone numbers?'

'I am.'

'Who supplied you?'

'I'm not going to tell you that.'

'It would help me greatly if I knew.'

'I've promised confidentiality.'

'How do I know it's reliable?'

'The source is guaranteed.'

'In other words it's his wife.'

George said nothing. He was glad not to be having this conversation face to face.

'If it was his wife,' said Sotiriou, 'she might well be suspected of seeking revenge on her husband for his affair with Mrs Boiatzis.'

George did not reply.

'I have no doubt that it is his wife,' Sotiriou continued. 'Who else would have access to his phone, who else would witness private visits late at night? Who else in the house would dare?'

George was damned if he would give the man the certainty he wanted. In any case he didn't like the question. Why did Sotiriou want to know the source? Was he really interested in checking its reliability? Or was he too in the pay of Kakridis?

'If I find you've been withholding evidence, Zafiris, you're going to be in trouble.'

'I've given you all the evidence.'

'But not the source!'

'You're not getting the source, and you know why.'

'If this goes wrong I'll lose my job, pension, everything.'

'You'll deserve to.'

'What the hell do you mean by that?'

'Anyone in your position who fails to make use of this evidence deserves to be fired. You've got an open goal in front of you. Put the ball in the fucking net!'

'It's not as simple as that.'

'If you want further evidence, tap *Kakridis'* phone.'

'Nice idea. I need permission from the Public Prosecutor for a phone tap, and I won't get that for a member of parliament without special permission from the minister responsible. Guess who that is.'

'Kakridis?'

'Correct!'

This was bad news. 'What are you going to do?'

Sotiriou waited a few seconds before replying. Then, in a weary, demoralised tone, he said, 'I'll look into it.'

Down at the Café Agamemnon Dimitri fixed him a fresh orange juice instead of his usual coffee. He wanted change in everything. The old routines felt like death. He flicked through the newspaper as he waited. A report on 'the new homeless' announced a twenty percent increase in people sleeping rough in Athens, many of them technical or professional people who had lost their jobs in the crisis. On another page, a group of the city's Muslims were pictured outside their improvised mosque – a basement near Omonia, where they prayed on a stained, damp carpet in an area cleared of packing cases and broken furniture. The doorway had been daubed with racist slogans. Their leader asked, 'When will the authorities let us build a proper mosque? We have the money, all we need is permission.' A local shopkeeper said, 'Let them go back to their own countries and pray. We had enough of Islam with four hundred years of the Turks.'

George turned to the sports pages and tried to read an article about the owners of Greek football teams. But his mind was soon back on his work.

He was uncertain about his next move. That was a blow about permission for the phone taps. Observing Kakridis any other way would be a nightmare.

He decided to call Pezas.

'Hector, I know you're a gadget man… I need some advice.'

'What's the problem?'

'Is there any way of bugging someone's mobile phone? Unofficially?'

Pezas hesitated. 'Unofficially, there is,' he said.

'Tell me.'

'You need to get hold of the target phone for a few minutes and load some software.'

'Is that easy to do?

'If you know how.'

'Invisible?'

'Completely.'

'What exactly does it do?'

'It makes the target phone transmit all conversations to another phone of your choice.'

'Every call, incoming and out?'

'Every call. It can also act as a room bug.'

'Without the user realising?'

'What the hell would be the point if the user realised?'

'Just checking.'

'Is it legal?'

'Not exactly.'

'Expensive?'

'It costs around 800 euros to buy.'

'Do you have one?'

'I do.'

'For hire?'

'250 a week, plus 600 deposit, returnable.'

'Nice return on investment.'

'We have to live.'

'Could you install it on Kakridis' phone?'

'He might have some kind of suppression or monitoring device.'

'And if he does?'

'It won't work. Quite apart from that it sounds risky.'

'Is it worth a try?'

'Possibly. How do we get to his phone?'

'His wife.'

'She'll have to install the software.'

'Is that a problem?'

'Women tend to be frightened of these things.'

'She's pretty sharp.'

Pezas seemed doubtful.

'What's the problem?' said George. 'You can show her how, presumably?'

'Yes of course.'

'So?'

'She mustn't get caught, that's all.'

'You say some very obvious things, Hector.'

31

The next morning's papers carried the story that Sophocles Ghiotis had recovered consciousness and dictated a message for his blog: 'They have not silenced me. Keep listening, keep talking, my friends. Never be afraid to speak the truth.' Apart from these stirring words, there was a brief announcement that he had been shot by unknown gunmen on Friday morning, but was now in a stable condition. Messages of support from listeners had been flooding in for the past three days.

George wondered who all these supporters might be. Ghiotis must be a hell of a performer. He did not seem the type to have 'friends' in the usual sense. On the other hand the city was full of people who felt cheated by the state, out of place in a culture of self-interest, people who longed for a society they could play a part in. These people existed in large numbers, but they were atomised, set against one another in futile antagonism. Ghiotis, rough-mannered as he was, offered them a community. Not a complete community, but better than none at all. In some ways it replicated the functions of the church, but without the physical contact, the traditions, the participation. Could Ghiotis heal injured spirits? Would he one day be enclosed in a silver casket and visited by pilgrims? Friend of the friendless, shepherd of lost souls?

George turned the pages of the newspaper. Queues at petrol stations around the country. A new strike by state employees. Papaconstantinou, the Minister of Finance, visiting Brussels and telling the world that Greece's economic reforms were on track. Papandreou, the Prime Minister, speaking on the island of Kastellorizo, asking the Greek people to be patient and resolute, not to fight against the inevitable. 'Our programme of change is necessary and non-negotiable. We cannot afford to fail.' Pensioners, students, workers saying, 'You've failed already! Stop punishing us for other people's dishonesty. Go to the rich for cash.'

George finished his coffee and climbed the stairs to his apartment. He rang Pezas to find out if Mrs Kakridis had managed to install the surveillance software in her husband's phone.

'She's done it,' said Hector. 'A model student.'

'Results?'

'Technically, good. We're hearing him loud and clear. But nothing interesting so far.'

'We must be patient.'

'Patient and resolute, as Papandreou says.'

He checked his laptop for emails. His inbox was the usual rubbish tip of bad jokes, investment ideas and offers of savings on fake Rolex watches and genital enhancements. In amongst them was a note from Abbas:

Strange happenings! The unpredictable nature of this country never fails to surprise me. Yesterday the colonel kindly offered me one of his rifles as a gift – to thank me for looking after him in prison: the lovely sporting Hämmerli that he used in the Olympics. An honour for me, which I am far from deserving. But here's the strange part: I've just been down to the police station to report the change of ownership. I expected this to be recorded in temporary form, given the absence of the firearms register. But no, the desk sergeant very calmly produced the old register! It's back! How or why I have no idea. I hid my astonishment as best I could. Somehow we must get our hands on it. I await your reply with barely suppressed impatience. Abbas.

George telephoned him at once.

'These people devote their lives to denying people's requests,' he said, 'so we'll have to be cunning. I'll come over to the island, and we'll go in to the police station together. I can be there at three. Will that suit you?'

'Fine,' said Abbas. 'I'll meet you off the ship.'

George shoved a few things into his briefcase and prepared to leave. His phone rang. He thought of ignoring it, then gave in. He could spare five minutes. It was Pezas.

'Listen to this,' he said.

Kakridis was talking to another man. Kakridis spoke first:

– You must have reserves.

– They're very low.

– You promised liquidity.

– Up to ten percent of invested funds. Conditional on…

– Don't give me that technical crap.

–… the state of the market. There was flow then. Now it's all dried up.

– Impossible!

– The season has barely started. Give it a chance.

– I have creditors. They don't have seasons.

– Tell them to wait.

– They don't do "wait".

– They're going to have to.

– How long?

– September, October.

– Impossible!

– You must have other sources.

– Not right now. This crisis is really fucking things up.

– We're all in it together.

– Look, are you sure you can't do two hundred?

– I can do fifty.

– Two hundred is the minimum.

– I can't.

– There's no such thing as can't.

– Oh yes there is.

– I've invested heavily with you.

– You're not the only one.

– Maybe not, but I'm a fucking big one!

– Listen, Byron, your friends must be patient. They know there's a crisis. The subsidies are drying up. We have to earn this money. Offer them a little extra in October. Explain about the season. Add three percent. That's not a bad rate of interest over a year.

– They're illiterates. Cash is paid on time and in full.

– Then you must borrow.

– Where?

– There's always someone with money to lend.

– God damn you!

The line went silent for a few moments. Then Pezas was asking him, 'What do you think?'

'Mildly squalid,' said George, 'but not incriminating. Who was he talking to?'

'Don't know yet.'

217

'Was that a call or a live conversation?'

'A call.'

'Where is he?'

'No idea. Could be anywhere.'

'Have you asked his wife?'

'No.'

'Try her. You might get something.'

George put down the phone, his mind unsettled by this conversation. Kakridis needed cash. Why? Who were these illiterate creditors? Were they the ones that worried his wife, or others? And who was this man who invested millions for him but could not advance two hundred thousand?

Kakridis was a powerful figure, immune from prosecution. Once a man like that knew where the evidence against him was collected, he could simply move in and have it destroyed: documents, recordings, photographs, computer files. Witnesses could be bribed or threatened. If George managed to get proof of any criminal activity, he would be at risk from the moment he tried to go public. Even if he went to the police he couldn't be sure of the consequences. Sotiriou seemed less and less to be trusted. The only policeman he knew he could rely on was Takis Mitropoulos, but he was out in the provinces, in a technical department, with no firepower against the establishment.

The press and media were the only other possibility, but few had the courage or energy of Ghiotis. Most of them were lapdogs, serving interests they didn't even understand.

George sat for a few minutes, his mind jammed with difficulties. Then he heard the church clock strike half past twelve. He snatched up his briefcase. He would miss the ferry if he didn't go.

*

Abbas was waiting on the quay: his tall, stooping figure clearly visible from the deck of the ship. He was shading himself from the sun with a newspaper, which he held above his head like a roof. They walked towards the police station, while George proposed his plan.

'I'll go in and say I've just had my pockets picked by a couple of Georgians. I'll keep the desk sergeant talking. Meanwhile you come in with a request to check the colonel's guns in the register. That will give you a pretext to go through and find the others on the list.'

'Identify them by their guns?'

'Exactly. My bet is that the Heckler & Koch will be missing. But you may as well get all the others. Or most of them. Do you have the two lists?'

'Of course.'

'Right, let's do it. Give me a couple of minutes' start.'

They parted at the end of the street that led to the police station. George walked through the doorway into the courtyard, along the flagstoned path beside the lemon trees and parked police cars. He entered the Officers' Room.

The desk sergeant was deeply absorbed in events on his computer screen, which may have been police business but sounded very like motor racing.

'I'd like to report a theft,' he said.

'Oh yes?' said the sergeant, turning down the angry insect sound of roaring engines but not taking his eyes off the screen.

'A couple of Georgians spotted me on the ship from Piraeus. They picked my pocket in the crowd as we came ashore.'

The sergeant did not appear to be listening.

'They stole three hundred and fifty euros. I want you to record this and give me a crime number.'

The sergeant reluctantly turned his attention to what George was saying.

'How many euros?'

'Three hundred and fifty.'

The policeman grimaced slightly, clicked a few times with his mouse, and said, 'Right. Theft report. Wednesday, thirtieth day of the sixth month. Year, 2010. Name and address?'

George answered all the questions, including his father's Christian name, his mother's maiden name, his date and place of birth, his marital status, occupation, tax number, and other irrelevant details. They moved on to the crime itself and a description of the perpetrators.

'Medium height,' said George. 'One ginger-haired, the other dark. Muscular, about thirty-five years old. Dressed in jeans and sports shirts.'

'Any beards, moustaches or side whiskers?'

'No.'

'Any scars or other distinguishing marks?'

'No.'

'You said they were Albanian?'

'Georgian.'

'How do you know?'

'I recognise the language.'

'How come?'

'I've had dealings with them before.'

'These particular men?'

'No. Other Georgians.'

Abbas walked in as the sergeant was noting down this information in slow and careful longhand. Speaking his odd, semi-grammatical Greek, Abbas explained what he was after. The sergeant, distracted by George, handed over the register and gestured for him to consult it on top of the counter where he could be clearly seen. Abbas opened the book, took some sheets of folded paper from his pocket and settled down to the job. George went steadily on with his story, describing the imaginary theft. From the corner of his eye he saw Abbas note down a name from time to time. He was working quickly, but there were still plenty of pages to go. The tale of the Georgians was almost done.

'Have you had problems with these people before?' asked George.

'No,' said the sergeant.

'You've heard about them, though?'

'I know they cause trouble in the cities.'

'Trouble? It's worse than that! No one's safe. They start protection rackets, backed up by a full programme of break-ins, arson and general intimidation. They have no scruples about killing. They have nothing to lose and plenty to gain.'

George watched the sergeant grow more alarmed as he laid on the detail.

'In Nea Smyrni they offered protection to the owner of a grocer's shop, one of those nice old-fashioned ones with barrels of feta and sacks of rice. The owner said no, I'm poor, I can't afford it. They took no notice. Burnt the place down within a week.'

'Mafia,' said the sergeant.

'Exactly!'

'What the hell do they want here?'

'They smell money. All those yachts in the harbour, the nice cafés. It's not a good sign when the Georgians appear.'

'This is a peaceful place.'

'It won't be much longer if they move in. You'll get protection rackets, gangs, drugs, the whole package.'

The sergeant looked pensive.

'I'll tell the boss. He will not be pleased to hear this!' He turned to Abbas. 'Finished yet?'

Abbas looked up. 'Very nearly.'

'It's not normally allowed,' said the sergeant.

'I'm most grateful to you,' said Abbas.

The sergeant lit a cigarette.

'Are we done?' asked George.

'Done,' said the sergeant, returning to his computer. 'You won't see your money again, but thanks for the warning.'

George met Abbas at a café a few minutes later. Abbas looked pleased with himself. He flattened the two lists of volunteers on the table, side by side.

'Here we are. Aeschylus, that's me. Daedalus is Paraskevás, the pilot…' He ran his index finger down the list. 'Look,' he said excitedly, 'I've got them. All but one. Leonidas, Nestor and Odysseus all had Mausers, so they must be Tasakos, Tsoublekas and Philippidis, it doesn't matter which. Doukakis has a Sarasqueta 12-bore so he must be Themistocles, and Socrates is the colonel. That leaves just Xenophon unaccounted for, and that can only be… I don't believe it. Kotsis! That's him!'

'The retired policeman?'

'Which explains how he was able to cut a page out of the register.'

George was troubled. 'I don't buy that. He told us he owned a Mauser.'

'He lied.'

'He showed us the gun! Don't you remember?'

'We don't know if that was his. And maybe he had two guns! The colonel has eight or nine.'

'He said he had registered the Mauser.'

'I didn't see it in the register. But it could have been on the missing page, with the Heckler & Koch.'

'Then why doesn't Xenophon have a Mauser as well as a Heckler & Koch on the list of volunteers?'

'The list could be incomplete. Or erroneous! Or drawn up before he acquired the Mauser...'

'Hold on, Abbas! My head's spinning.'

'Forget the lists. Kotsis had two guns, OK? The Mauser and the HK. He showed us the Mauser, and kept quiet about the HK. It's as simple as that.'

'But three others also had Mausers.'

'They're irrelevant.'

'So why isn't Xenophon one of those three?'

'Because they're all in the police register. He's the only one missing. It has to be him.'

'I still don't believe it. He seemed a totally decent man.'

'He is a decent man. I know him and like him. But something made him open his window one evening and shoot poor old Professor Petrakis in the head.'

'Why in heaven's name would he do that?'

'That is the million-dollar question! We have to go and ask him.'

George needed to check the reasoning again before he would accept this. He leaned over the table, shielding his eyes from the glare of the street, and ran his eye down the lists, comparing the information, repeating the names out loud. Finally he sat back in his chair, his brain struggling with the inevitable conclusion.

'You're right,' he said. 'It has to be Kotsis.'

'Are you ready to confront him?'

'We might as well. The police will never get round to it.'

They rang the bell at the retired policeman's house and waited. Pigeons burbled in the vine leaves above the gate. A scooter buzzed past, swerving around a dog sleeping in the dust. At last the gate was opened by Mrs Kotsis.

'Come in,' she said. 'Welcome, Abbas. And Mr… I've forgotten your name.'

'Zafiris.'

'Come in. What can I offer you?'

'We're fine,' said Abbas. 'We need to see Leonardos. Is he in?'

'He's sleeping.'

'Would you mind waking him?'

This was such an unusual request that she sensed trouble.

'What's happened?' she asked, without moving from the gateway.

'We need to talk to him urgently,' said Abbas.

'Something with the colonel?'

'Just bring him, please.'

She showed them through a door into the yard.

'There are chairs under the trees,' she said.

They passed from the shadow of the hallway to the hot dazzle of the yard, where the sun had been baking the concrete all day. At the far side the fruit trees cast a cool pall of shade. They found chairs and sat in silence, waiting.

Kotsis appeared, puffy-eyed, frowning, his hair freshly slicked down with water.

'Gentlemen, how can I help you?'

'You remember Mr Zafiris?' said Abbas.

He did.

'We have a difficult matter to discuss with you,' said Abbas.

'Tell me.'

'George, will you explain?'

George hesitated a moment, then plunged in.

'When we last spoke, I asked if you had a rifle. You showed me a German Army Mauser.'

'Yes.'

'You didn't say you had another gun.'

'I don't.'

George paused. He needed to stay calm, and give the man a chance to tell the truth.

'Perhaps you don't have a second rifle now, but did you have one earlier this year?'

The policeman's eyes showed a momentary flicker of uncertainty.

'No,' he said. 'Not this year.'

'Are you quite sure?'

'I'm sure.'

OK, thought George, you deserve what's coming.

'I have reason to believe you're lying.'

The policeman shrugged. 'I'm sorry about that. What can I do to convince you?'

'Why not tell the truth?'

'I've told you.'

'Mr Kotsis, I happen to know that a Heckler & Koch G3 was registered in your name as well as the Mauser.'

'A Heckler & Koch?'

'That's right.'

'When was that?'

'1990.'

The policeman seemed puzzled. 'Twenty years ago!'

'Is that important?'

'You didn't ask me about guns I used to own. I'd forgotten about it.'

'That's odd, because that very gun was on the page of the

police firearms register which you removed.'

'I removed?'

'Yes! You removed.'

'I haven't been near that register for years.'

'Maybe someone did it for you? Bagatzounis? His sergeant? It doesn't matter. The evidence was tampered with. That alone is enough to put you in prison.'

'Why would I remove a page from the register?'

'You know as well as I do.'

'I don't!'

'All right, I'll explain. The Heckler & Koch was the weapon that killed John Petrakis. The page was removed so that your link with the weapon could not be traced.'

'How do you know all this?'

'I've seen the ballistics report. And you own the only G3 on the island!'

'I once owned it.'

'Why is there no trace of this in the firearms register?'

'I have no idea.'

'Because you, or someone at your request, cut out the relevant page!'

'Mr Zafiris, you're talking about a document we can't see.'

'OK, let's get back to the facts. You once owned this weapon?'

'Twenty years ago.'

'What did you do with it?'

'I gave it away.'

'To?'

Another tiny flicker of uncertainty.

'To a relative.'

'Was the change of ownership recorded in the firearms register?'

'I can't remember. I expect it was. I like to do things correctly.'

'When did you give the gun away?'

'Soon after I bought it.'

'Why?'

'I used it a few times and decided it wasn't for me.'

'So this relative took it. And kept it?'

'He kept it. For how long I can't say.'

'Where did he live?'

'In Athens.'

'Why would he want a rifle in Athens?'

'He went hunting at weekends.'

'Where is this relative now?'

The policeman hesitated. 'Is this going to lead to an accusation of murder?'

'If he had the gun on March 25th, I'm afraid it is.'

Kotsis looked appalled. He seemed overcome. Unable to speak, he simply shook his head. His eyes filled with tears.

'Do you think your relative would have had any reason to shoot Professor Petrakis?' asked George.

'No,' whispered Kotsis.

'Perhaps he can tell us himself?'

Kotsis did not reply. George waited, watching him.

'Do you think he can tell us?' he asked again.

Kotsis seemed tongue-tied.

'Your old friend Colonel Varzalis has been accused of this murder,' said George. 'He has spent many days in prison. He's innocent. The killer has to be found.'

'My relative isn't capable of killing anyone,' said Kotsis.

'Will you tell me his name?'

Kotsis stood up. 'I'll be back in a moment.'

George turned to Abbas. 'Do you know who he's talking

about?'

'No.'

'Is he telling the truth?'

They heard a cry from the house. Then Mrs Kotsis shouting, 'Don't Leo, don't do that!'

Her husband's conciliatory reply was too soft to hear. It was followed at once by a shout of 'You'll kill us all!'

Kotsis came out a short while later. 'I've spoken to my brother-in-law,' he said. 'I'll take you to see him.'

They followed Kotsis to a house a few streets away, where the door was opened to them by an exhausted woman in a nightdress. She was bulbously overweight and pale, her hair greasy and unwashed.

'Hello, Leonardo,' she said dully.

'I've come to see Manos.'

'He's on his way. Come in.'

They entered the house, forced to move sideways through the entrance hall, which was piled high with black plastic rubbish sacks full of clothes, video tapes, old newspapers and magazines.

'Go into the lounge,' said the woman.

Kotsis led them into a dark, heavily overfurnished room, with sofas and armchairs so crowded together that there was barely room to sit. He tried the light switch, but it was dead.

'I'll open the shutters,' he said, and made for the window. A large dining table in a logjam of chairs and sofas blocked his way.

'To hell with it,' said Kotsis, 'we'll leave the door open.'

As their eyes adjusted to the half-light, George noted the strange array of objects that cluttered the room: china statuettes, an old radio, a pair of hairdryers from a professional salon, a food mixer, piles of books and CDs, baskets, suitcases, skis, a basketball net on a stand, a bed on its side. All jumbled and out of use. It made no sense as a room.

The woman left them alone. The air was hot and musty. Kotsis squeezed himself into an armchair and sat down, an expression of hopelessness on his face.

The light from the doorway flickered.

Manos Tasakos walked in.

'We've come –' George began, but Kotsis interrupted.

'The weapon that killed Petrakis has been traced. It was the Heckler & Koch I gave you.'

Tasakos said nothing.

'What happened?' asked Kotsis.

'I was in Athens on March 25th,' said Tasakos. 'I've already explained that to the detective.'

'You have witnesses?'

'Of course.'

'OK, so it wasn't you. But someone used your rifle to kill the professor!'

'I don't know…'

'What the hell do you mean you don't know? It was your gun! Tell us what happened!'

'I wasn't here, Leo! What can I say?'

'Tell the truth! Get it out so we can deal with it!'

'I did not fire that gun.'

'Who did?'

'How should I know?'

'Was it Maria? Was it Stelios? Lydia? Who?'

'Leo, you can see the situation here. We're in a mess. Nothing works. Maria takes a kilo of pills every day and she's like a zombie. Stelios is in a world of his own, and who can blame him? Lydia's a martyr who only stays with us to become a saint, and I'm trying to keep this catastrophe afloat by running a business.'

'A man was killed. Shot with your gun. You have to face this! You have to explain it!'

'I can't! How can anyone explain it? It's just one more piece of shit in this great shithouse of a life!'

'The police will come, Manos. They'll arrest you. You'll go to prison. Your business will fail and your family will no longer be protected.'

'I wasn't here! I was in Athens!'

Kotsis gave him a few moments' respite, then returned to the attack.

'They've traced the gun to this house. Someone in this house…'

'Can't you just leave us alone!'

'Of course I can. We all can. But the police can't. They're going to come and …'

'They've already got a killer. Varzalis is a fascist, a queer-hater, an extremist. He's been killing all his life.'

'He's innocent!'

'He has the perfect motive.'

'He didn't do it.'

'So you say!'

'What about the gun?'

'Maybe he came round here and borrowed it? How do I know?'

Abbas said, 'We all counted ourselves as his friends at one time. We all served with the volunteers.'

'Volunteers! Boy scouts!'

'Don't take out your frustrations on him,' said Kotsis.

Tasakos was angry now. 'The colonel's a vegetable. He's no use now. His life's over. Let him go to prison. He won't even know he's in there.'

'Whoever killed Petrakis has to face the consequences.'

'I've thrown the guns in the sea. All of them. It won't happen again.'

'If it's not the guns it will be something else. A knife. A pillow. A hammer. It's not weapons that cause crime, Manos!'

Tasakos had his head in his hands.

'Just tell us,' said Kotsis. 'Get it out and over with.'

Tasakos was weeping. 'I can't,' he said. 'You must go. Please. Leave us alone.'

'The police will come.'

'Let them come. I don't care. They won't find anything… I can't stand this any more.'

Kotsis sat still and watched him.

Tasakos raised his head. His face was burning with pain.

'I told you to go! Get the hell out of my house!'

'We're not going until you tell us what happened.'

'I don't know what happened! I came back from Athens that night and someone said there had been a shooting. Life was going on as normal here. Maria in a haze, Lydia preparing food, Stelios buried in his computer.'

'Did you check your guns?'

'No.'

'Why not?'

'I had no reason to.'

'So why did you throw your guns in the sea?'

Tasakos shrugged his shoulders. 'I didn't want to take any chances.'

'You must have had a reason.'

Tasakos sighed. 'No! I just took the guns and the ammunition and threw the whole damn lot in the sea.'

'And then you cut a page out of the police register?'

Tasakos said nothing.

The four men sat in silence. George had let Kotsis do all the questioning. But there was an important question he had not yet asked.

'Did you check with the members of your household to see if anyone had touched your gun?'

Tasakos threw him a despairing look, then said softly, 'No.'

'Why not?'

Tasakos leaned back in his chair and closed his eyes.

Kotsis signalled to George not to pursue the matter.

Having remained silent for much of this painful conversation, Abbas now spoke.

'I don't know who did this,' he said, 'but I have an idea. I want to remind us all of the vow we made one night with the colonel, as his volunteers. What did we swear to do? To uphold the law, and make life better in this tormented land… Do you remember that?'

'That's easy to say,' Tasakos retorted. 'But when it comes to sacrificing your own family…'

'I simply ask if you remember that oath.'

'I remember,' said Kotsis.

'Did we believe it? I did! We all did, or we wouldn't have been there, losing half a night's sleep, stumbling about among the rocks and the thorns! Were we right or wrong to believe it? You can't vow to uphold the law and allow a member of your family to murder an innocent man!'

Tasakos suddenly erupted, 'It was not murder!'

'It most certainly was!'

'Murder is premeditated. You have to know what you're doing. You have to intend to kill.'

'So what was this? An accident?'

'No. It's… I don't know the word.'

Kotsis said, 'It is murder, but with diminished responsibility. If the court accepts that the person who committed the crime is mentally unstable.'

Tasakos had closed his eyes again. He breathed heavily, shaking his head as if to rid it of its appalling thoughts. Kotsis watched him carefully.

After a time, Kotsis spoke. He was calm and businesslike.

'I'm going to suggest a plan. You and I, Manos, know who fired the gun. The police don't know, but a few questions will lead even a blockhead like Bagatzounis to the inevitable conclusion. Arrest, trial, psychiatric assessments will follow. There's no way of avoiding that. In addition you will be found guilty of destroying evidence and obstructing the course of justice. This will make a bad situation worse. If you go to prison your family is in ruins. Who will look after Maria? What will happen to Stelios? Who'll run the business? Where will Lydia go with no one to pay her wages? Who will maintain the house, pay the bills? So let's accept the inevitable and do our best to limit the damage. Go to the police, Manos! Tell them the truth. Help them. Get this mess sorted out, and with luck they'll find a way to overlook the business with the register.'

'I've told you, I don't know who fired the gun.'

'You know damn well, and so do I. And if Abbas hasn't guessed by now he's not the man I took him for.'

Tasakos seemed fired by a sudden resolution. 'Look, we can keep this to ourselves. Zafiris is a businessman, I'll make it worth his while. And we also made a vow, Abbas, to defend each other. Have you forgotten that?'

Abbas shook his head. 'Count me out, Manos.'

'What? You'd go to the police?'

'I'd go to the police if it was my own brother. I don't want to get shot when I'm watering my garden, or wake up one night and find my house on fire.'

'That won't happen. I've talked to him.'

'He's not well, Manos!' said Kotsis.

'He understands!'

'He has no idea! If he's capable of doing it once, he's capable of doing it again. Especially if he gets away with it!'

'He won't. He's promised.'

'He will, Manos. It's a certainty.'

'Why don't you help me, Leo, instead of persecuting me?'

Kotsis returned his brother-in-law's gaze with tormented sympathy.

'Well?' demanded Tasakos. 'Are you in or not?'

'I've told you what to do, Manos.'

'So you're out! My own family!'

'Even if you convinced them, you wouldn't convince me,' said George.

'I'll make it worth your while… What do you want? Half a million?'

'I can't do that.'

'Seven fifty! You can retire on that!'

'No.'

'What's your problem?'

'Abbas said it. There's no point repeating it.'

'I'm offering you three quarters of a million euros!'

'I heard you.'

Tasakos leaned forward aggressively, eyes blazing. 'Any bank account, anywhere in the world!'

George had no desire to humiliate the man – loathsome, desperate as he was.

'If you have that kind of money,' he said, 'you should spend it on getting the best possible treatment for your wife and son.'

Tasakos exploded. 'What the hell do you know about my

wife and son? Have you come here to insult my family?'

'Leave him alone, Manos!' said Kotsis. 'He's right. We're all agreed.'

'And you're a fucking traitor!'

'If you don't go to the police with us right now, we're going without you.'

'Traitor!'

'Decide.'

'Traitor!'

Kotsis stood up. 'Gentlemen, let's go.'

They walked to the police station through streets glowing with crimson light, a strange dreamlike tension in the air, as if a storm was hovering. As they entered the Officers' Room, the desk sergeant saw Kotsis and stood up at once, with an eagerness that George would not have thought him capable of.

'Good evening, Inspector!' he said.

'Hello, Taso. Everything all right?'

'Fine, thank you! What brings you here, sir?'

'I need to see Bagatzounis. Is he still here?'

'He's in his office. Shall I tell him?'

'No need.'

Kotsis knocked at the station commander's door. An irritable croak came through in reply, and Kotsis turned the handle. Bagatzounis welcomed him with an enthusiastic smile, which faded rapidly when he saw who was with him.

'Serious business, Themis, I'll get straight to the point. We've just come from my brother-in-law's house.'

'Ah,' said Bagatzounis. His face assumed a sympathetic, toadying look. 'How are things?'

'Worse than you can imagine.'

'Oh? Why?'

'His son shot that professor.'

'Stelios?'

Kotsis nodded.

'My God,' said Bagatzounis. 'After all they've been through.'

'I know. It's cruel.'

'Is he going to come in?'

'I don't know. He's in shock.'

'Are you sure about this?'

'No question. Manos owned the weapon, his son used it.'

'Can we go back a stage? How do you know about the gun?'

'It was mine! I gave it to Manos.'

'No! I mean how do you know that was the weapon used to kill?'

'It's in the forensic report,' said George.

'Really?' said Bagatzounis. 'And how do we know about that?'

'I have my sources. Feel free to check the accuracy of what I'm saying.'

'I have to say I find this utterly improper.'

'Listen,' said Kotsis, 'Zafiris is right. He traced the HK to me, and through me to Manos. There's no mistake. Manos has more or less admitted everything.'

'So what do I do?'

'Go and see him. Take a statement.'

'Now?'

'Yes. Now for heaven's sake!'

Bagatzounis seemed lost. 'This is a serious case,' he said, half to himself. 'It'll be taken over by Piraeus, the Violent Crimes Unit… I have no influence at all up there.'

'Just tell them the background. Ask them to treat these

people decently.'

Bagatzounis glanced at George. 'What about this gentleman here?'

'Ask him!' said Kotsis.

Bagatzounis pursed his lips, and brought the finger tips of both hands together. 'Mr Zafiris,' he said, 'I believe I made it clear from the start that the police are in no position to pay a reward for any information…'

'All you made clear, Captain, was that you were unwilling to help or be helped.'

'Precisely! Police business is police business.'

'I'm being paid privately.'

'This must not go to the press.'

'What do you take me for?'

'I must point out the delicate nature…'

'Don't worry, Captain. I understand.'

'This is a family, a good family, that has suffered untold difficulties!'

'You can rely on my discretion.'

Bagatzounis seemed relieved.

George continued: 'But if this case gets bogged down in bureaucratic procedures, and I hear that Stelios is still at liberty, I'll take this to a higher authority.'

Bagatzounis held up his hand. 'There will be no need for that.'

'Come on,' said Kotsis. 'Let's get this over with.'

In company with Bagatzounis, they walked back through the town to the Tasakos house.

'I hoped you wouldn't come,' said Manos.

'I wish we didn't have to,' said Bagatzounis mournfully. 'Is your son at home?'

'He's in his room.'

'Will you call him down?'

They waited at the open doorway, unsettled by the rubbish-strewn hall and its wafts of damp, stale air.

Tasakos returned with his son, a tall, bearded, overweight young man who could be anything from seventeen to thirty years old. Pale and expressionless, his eyes flickered from face to face without recognition.

'Hello, young man,' said Kotsis with an effort at brightness.

'Hello, uncle.'

'This is Captain Bagatzounis. He took over from me as chief of police. He needs to ask you some questions.'

'OK.'

'Not here in the street,' said Bagatzounis.

'Where then?' asked Stelios.

'It has to be done properly, with a voice recorder and a witness. And you have the right to be represented by a lawyer.'

'A lawyer? What's this about?'

'A shooting which took place on March 25th.'

'I don't know anything about it.'

'I don't think that's true.'

'It is true!'

'Come with me to the police station.'

'No thanks.'

'You have to make a statement.'

'I've told you it's not true.'

'That's not enough. I need to question you properly according to the law. For that you must come to the station.'

'Colonel Varzalis did it.'

'Oh God, not you too!' said Abbas.

'Let's stop wasting time,' said Kotsis. 'Go with the captain, just go.'

The young man's eyes became agitated. 'I don't have to,' he said.

'You have no choice.'

'Let me get my laptop.'

'No. You don't need your laptop to answer a few questions.'

'I need it for other things.'

'Other things must wait.'

'They're urgent!'

'Only one thing's urgent now…'

Bagatzounis stepped forward. Nervously, his hands shaking, he forced a pair of handcuffs onto the young man's wrists.

32

On the deck of the *Aghios Nektarios*, cutting its pale furrow through the dark sea, George felt strangely dissatisfied. He had found the killer, but there was no sense of fulfilment in the work. Justice had not been done – only a series of injustices. The young man that killed John Petrakis seemed disconnected from his act. He showed no awareness, no responsibility, no regret. Did he even know what he was doing when he pulled the trigger? That a mechanism was released, a spring-loaded pin struck the centre of a cartridge, an explosion occurred in that tiny brass chamber and a cone of lead began spinning through the air, crossing the space between two buildings in a tenth of a second, flying straight and true until it found an obstacle in the skull of the professor? Broke through the skin and bone, ploughed on through his brain, driving a bow wave of splinters and shredded tissues before it, dragging a vortex of blood and pulped grey matter behind? Did he sense any of that? That a life was ended at that moment, a brilliant life, while his own existence continued, gaining nothing, feeling nothing, learning nothing?

The waste upset him most. Petrakis had been an apostle of freedom. Stelios was a slave of forces he would never understand. Behind that tragedy lay other tragedies – his mother's blasted existence, the father's ruined hopes, untold miseries in previous generations. What hope could there be for any of them?

He thought of contacting Constantine Petrakis. He wanted to hear the man's reaction when he told him who had killed his brother. But he'd had enough for one day.

The ship sailed into the harbour at Piraeus. A glittering web of electric light drew them in. Dirty pink and yellow, like an unwashed wound. He walked off the ramp into the chaos of cars and foot passengers, crossed the street and headed towards the railway station, thinking of home, a glass of wine, food and bed.

As he stepped onto the train his phone rang.

It was Pezas, in a high state of excitement.

'Where are you, George?'

'Piraeus. Just getting on the train home.'

'Don't go home. Stay on the train up to Kifissia.'

'Why?'

'There's something going on at the Kakridis house.'

'What sort of thing?'

'The Georgians are there.'

'Yes?'

'They're giving him a hard time.'

'He probably deserves it.'

'His wife wants us to go over.'

'That's not a good idea. She should call the police.'

'She doesn't want to do that.'

'He's a government minister! Where's his security?'

'I don't know. He must have sent them away.'

'He's an idiot. A total bloody idiot... Listen, George, where's his wife?'

'At the house.'

'Tell her to leave.'

'I've tried that. She won't.'

'Don't go there yourself.'

'We can't just abandon her!'

'If she won't follow instructions, we can.'

'She's employing us, George!'

'Not as bodyguards. Call the police!'

'No.'

'Then I will.'

'Don't!'

'We haven't had this conversation. I'm calling them.'

'Don't, George!'

'Why the hell not?'

'It'll destroy her husband's career.'

'And about time!'

'George, please don't do it. Not yet. Just get yourself over here.'

In the chaos of thoughts that invaded his mind was a sudden suspicion. 'You're not seeing her, are you?'

'What do you mean?'

'Involved with her?'

'No way!'

'Where are you?'

'In Kefalari.'

'Promise me you won't go into the house.'

'It's OK, I'm in the street.'

'I'll be there as soon as I can.'

George hung up, thinking he should take a taxi instead of the train. Pezas needed help quickly. He stood up, heard the buzzer for the closing doors, and hurried off the train.

He found a cab on Akti Miaouli and gave the address in Kefalari. He hoped the driver would keep quiet. It was a distant hope, but sometimes you were lucky. He closed his eyes and tried to rest.

They were approaching Syntagma Square when his phone

rang. It was Pezas again, speaking softly, his voice tense.

'We've been listening in, using his phone. The Georgians are getting heavy now, saying pay or else.'

'So what's new?'

'He says he can't pay till after the summer.'

'What do they say?'

'They won't wait. They want valuables. Paintings, jewellery, antiques. Kakridis is saying don't be stupid, you'll only get a quarter of their value if you sell them. You know what the Georgian guy said? Thanks for the tip. We'll take four times as much.'

'Fair enough.'

'Kakridis didn't like that, but he's – oh no… hold on!'

The phone was silent for a few moments. Then Pezas was back. 'They've started taking paintings off the walls. Mrs K is going crazy. She wants to go in and stop them.'

'Tell her not to.'

'She wants me to go with her.'

'Don't, Hector, it's too risky.'

'I know. She won't listen.'

'Then let her go!'

'I can't.'

'Stay where you are, Hector! You've seen these guys in action. They don't give a shit.'

'Oh hell, she's off!'

'Let her go.'

The phone went dead.

George swore. Pezas was being a fool, but he suspected that in his place he would have done the same.

They were on Leoforos Kifissias now, about twenty minutes away, but the traffic was moving slowly. As they came to Faros, Pezas rang again.

'We're inside the gate now, watching the house. It's all quite calm. No one's talking. I guess the Georgians are helping themselves…'

'Where's Mrs Kakridis?'

'She's with me.'

'Can you ask her something for me?'

'What?'

'Who was her husband with this morning, when he was asking for money? You remember, you relayed the conversation to me?'

'Didn't I tell you?'

'No. Tell me now!'

'Hang on, I can see the front door opening now. There's a man coming out, carrying paintings…'

'Who was he talking to? '

There was no reply from Pezas. George heard Mrs Kakridis say, 'I'm going to talk to him,' and Pezas say 'Don't!' Then, 'Oh Jesus, she's going.'

'She's crazy,' said George.

'She's shouting at the Georgian. He's stopped… No, he's going towards the Mercedes. Now he's resting the paintings on the ground, he's opening the boot of the car. But she's come up and grabbed the paintings. He's seen her and called someone else… She's walking into the house with the two pictures. A man's come out, a big man blocking the doorway. She's telling him to get out of the way. He's not budging. She's shouting at him and trying to get past him. He's raised his… oh no, he's hit her! She's down! He's picked up the paintings and he's taking them back to the car. But she's up and after him. I don't like this, George! He's turned to face her – he's dropped the paintings – she's shouting at him, they've grabbed her arms, they've got her up against the car… Jesus, man this is bad, I've got to stop it!'

'Hector, don't!'

'I'm going to put a bullet up their asses!'

The phone went dead.

George called the police. Never mind what Mrs Kakridis had said, the situation was out of control. He told a duty officer to send an emergency team over to the minister's house as fast as possible.

George asked the taxi driver how long to go.

'Ten minutes,' he said.

It was probably nine and a half minutes too long.

*

For once the police had moved quickly. There were two squad cars parked in the street, two up at the house, red and blue lights flashing along the white stucco of the wall. A young policeman stood on guard at the gate.

George paid off the taxi and asked to be let through.

'You can't go in, sir.'

'I'm a friend of Mrs Kakridis.'

'No public are allowed in, sir.'

'She called me to come and help.'

'You can't go in.'

'What's happened?'

'I can't tell you.'

'Oh, for heaven's sake, she called me! My friend Hector Pezas is in there too. We're private detectives, working for her, trying to protect her.'

'It's too late for that.'

'Why? What's happened?'

'She's been shot.'

'What about Pezas?'

'There are four bodies.'

'Four?'

He suddenly felt sick.

'We're just trying to establish who's who,' said the policeman.

'Maybe I can help?' said George.

'If you know them…'

'What about Kakridis?'

'Minister Kakridis is safe.'

Of course he is, the bastard, thought George.

'There was a robbery going on and someone called the police.'

'I called the police,' said George, 'and it wasn't a robbery.'

'What was it?'

'Debt collection.'

'I'm sorry?'

'Never mind. Can I go up to the house?'

'Do you have some ID?'

George showed his card and was allowed through.

The bodies were lying like fingers on a hand, half in shadow, half in the light that spilled from the porch. Mrs Kakridis lay face down, a pulpy mess of bloodstained hair at the base of her skull. Behind her, lying partly across her legs, was the 'big man'. He too had his face to the ground, a crimson stain between his shoulder blades. Head to head with him was another man, who had fallen on his side. He looked as if he was asleep. A short distance away, behind the big man, their feet almost touching, lay Pezas, on his back, mouth and eyes open, gaping at the night sky. He had taken two bullets in his chest.

George stopped, paralysed by the sight of his friend. All he could think was, 'Stupid idiot! Why the hell didn't you listen to me?'

He glanced around. Police officers were photographing, discussing, dictating notes into miniature recording machines. On a balcony to the left of the porch he saw Kakridis, pacing and talking energetically into a phone.

George knew there was something missing… The Mercedes. It should be here, unless it had got away. He scanned the garden. Up against the perimeter wall, to the right of the house, he spotted a dark shape. He walked over. As he came closer he saw that it was a car, parked oddly. In fact it wasn't parked at all, it was stopped, with its front end buried in the garden wall. A figure was collapsed over the steering wheel. George shone the light of his torch over him: he too had been shot, with a wound in the neck that must have sliced the carotid artery. The man's left shoulder, his arms, his entire torso glistened with blood. So, thought George, Pezas got three of them.

A new police car swung into the drive, its headlights sweeping across the garden. As it pulled up, a rear door opened and Sotiriou stepped out. Kakridis glanced at the new arrival, nodded, and carried on with his phone call.

Sotiriou went straight over to the four bodies, knelt by each one in turn, and said something to an assistant which George could not catch.

Kakridis finished his phone call and vanished from the balcony. A few seconds later he appeared at the front door. He hesitated a moment, then moved slowly down the steps towards Sotiriou.

George was thirty metres away, out beyond the lights. He could not hear their conversation. He noticed that Kakridis had lost his arrogant bearing. He seemed to have aged twenty years. They stood talking, their eyes fixed on the bodies at their feet.

Sotiriou raised his head and caught sight of the Mercedes against the garden wall. He began to walk towards it, Kakridis following.

They had not seen George. Or if they had, they hadn't registered who he was. They walked past him, enveloped in their conversation.

'Is that your car?' asked Sotiriou.

'No,' said Kakridis.

'What were these people doing here?' asked Sotiriou.

'They were stealing paintings.'

'Who let them in?'

'My wife.'

'Did she know them?'

'They claimed to be art collectors. Clients of the gallery.'

'Where were you when the shooting happened?'

'In my study.'

'Doing what?'

'Talking to one of these men. The one who's sitting in the car now.'

'About what?'

'What the hell do you think? I was telling him to get off my property!'

'Then what happened?'

'We heard shouts. He ran out, I followed, there was shooting… By the time I got out here I saw this.'

'So they weren't art collectors?'

'No way.'

'You've never met them before?'

'Never!'

'Why did they start shooting?'

'I have no idea.'

'So, there's one in the car, three on the ground, your wife…'

Kakridis threw up his hands. 'God knows who, how many…'

'One of the men down there is a private detective,' said Sotiriou. 'His name is Hector Pezas.'

Kakridis did not react.

'What was he doing here?'

'I wish I knew.'

'Did you know him?'

'No.'

'Did your wife know him?'

'She never mentioned his name.'

'How did he get in?'

'I don't know.'

They walked slowly up to the porch.

George waited on the lawn. The ease and fluency of Kakridis's lying was incredible. He could invent fictions even in a state of shock. A true professional. He walked towards the house.

Sotiriou saw George first. He did not seem pleased.

'Mr Zafiris? Have you just arrived?'

'About ten minutes ago.'

'What brings you here?'

'Hector Pezas called me.'

Kakridis looked up and recognised him with a start.

'Hector called me when he saw this trouble starting,' said George. 'He went to help. Against my advice.'

'What was he doing here?' asked Sotiriou.

'He was working for Mrs Kakridis. We both were.'

'In what capacity?'

George began to explain.

'Mother of God!' Kakridis broke in. 'Why are we listening to this?'

'We should let him have his say,' said Sotiriou.

'She didn't let these men in,' said George. 'Mr Kakridis did. He knew them and had dealings with them.'

'Bullshit!' said Kakridis. 'And this man has been trying to blackmail me for the last month.'

'Nothing of the kind, Mr Kakridis! I came to help a friend, who died trying to save your wife. And she died trying to save you!'

'Leave my property, Mr Detective! Your lies aren't wanted here!'

'We'll see who's lying,' said George.

Sotiriou eyed the two men sceptically.

'I'm going to ask you both to make sworn statements,' he said.

'Fuck your sworn statements,' said Kakridis. 'This man is a liar, a blackmailer, and a shit. He'll have no problem swearing to any libellous crap that passes though his head.'

'Just get the transcripts of our phone conversations,' said George. 'Mine and Hector's. There's enough in there to back up everything I've said.'

'Get out!' shouted Kakridis.

George stood his ground. 'When you discover who these "art collectors" are, you'll see that Mr Kakridis has been doing business with them for some time now, commissioning work…'

Kakridis raised his fist. 'Get out of here before I kill you.'

Sotiriou took George by the elbow and urged him to leave.

'Pay your bills, Mr Kakridis!' he shouted. 'The Georgians will be back. Who'll protect you then?'

Sotiriou propelled him away.

'Kakridis is lying,' he said. 'Get those transcripts. Listen to the conversations.'

'We need an order from the Public Prosecutor.'

'For a phone tap, surely not a transcript?'

'It comes to the same thing. Invasion of privacy.'

'I give you full permission to transcribe my calls.'

'What about Hector?'

'He's dead!'

'That complicates it even more. He can no longer give permission for his part of the conversation to be made public. So it has to go to the Prosecutor.'

'OK, let it go to the Prosecutor!'

'He won't take it on. The minister is immune from prosecution. You know that. It takes a special parliamentary committee…'

'Oh God! Here we go again!'

'Have you no more evidence than that?'

'The only one with more is Ghiotis.'

'He died this afternoon.'

'No! So this bastard gets away.'

'I can't take this any further,' said Sotiriou. 'Until I get some hard evidence, not from the phone, I'm stuck.'

'Do you at least believe what I'm telling you?'

'I have to keep an open mind.'

'Talk to those two hoodlums who whacked my place. They're part of this.'

'We will. Their testimony will be suspect, of course…'

George threw up his hands.

'OK. I give up. Let the bastard carry on, and I hope he kills one of your friends next.'

'I'm sorry about Hector,' said Sotiriou ruefully.

They had reached the gate.

'I'd better get back now,' he said at last. 'Go home, Zafiris. Try to forget this.'

'I'm going,' said George.

*

It was a warm night, scented with jasmine from the gardens along the street, with gusts of thyme from the wild land opposite. Ahead, the lights of Kifissia glowed, with the cypresses of the cemetery silhouetted against an opalescent sky. Soon Hector would be in the earth. George would have to find another man to help with gadgets and difficult days. The thought of him dead was sickening, unreal, and unjust beyond belief. Pangs of sorrow and pity twisted through him. But Hector had gone into the dark, and there was no calling him back.

As he walked towards Kifissia, past gleaming jeeps and executive cars, armoured gates with sensor lights and security cameras, past high stone walls that hid immense villas, he thought with bitterness of Kakridis, the shark who had surfaced just briefly from the waters where he usually hunted. George had almost netted him. But almost wasn't good enough. He had slipped away at the last moment, back into the slimy black world of menace, corruption and bought loyalty. There he would continue to survive until a beast even more vicious and unscrupulous than himself came along one day and destroyed him. Whether that was a Georgian killer or an Athenian policeman scarcely mattered now. The Georgians, being more organised and determined, would probably get him first. It was only a question of time.

Epilogue

Six weeks later, in mid-August, George was in Andros. His life had slowed to an easy summer pace. Swimming, eating, a few errands in town. He managed to forget, for hours at a stretch, the bad time he had been through. Then something would remind him – a remark, a colour, a scent, a sudden image in his mind's eye – and he was back in Kefalari, with four bodies on the ground and a black Mercedes, a corpse at the wheel, smashed into a garden wall.

One morning the postman brought a letter from Aegina, the name and address on the envelope a little masterpiece of calligraphy. He opened it, glanced at the first few lines, and flipped to the signature: Abbas. He turned it over again and read slowly from the beginning.

Dear George,

After you left the island a few puzzles remained in my mind. The arrest of Stelios Tasakos was far from settling everything. The doubts and uncertainties continued to nag me until at last I had to put a hold on the rest of my life and find some answers.

Question: why did Leonardos Kotsis try so hard to protect Stelios? Answer: the boy is his nephew.

There is more to this family business than meets the eye. Kotsis, Tasakos, Yerakas, Kakridis, Petrakis: a line of blood and marriage runs through this story like an underground river of which we were unaware. Everyone is related to everyone else. They look out for each other, they have circuits of protection and loyalty which are invisible to outsiders. Hurt one and you hurt them all.

Yerakas, Kakridis and Petrakis are not just relatives but business partners. Yerakas handles the projects and finance. Kakridis clears the political pathways for their ventures, and Petrakis does the legal work. They make a formidable team. The attempt to blame Colonel Varzalis for the death of John Petrakis was motivated by family solidarity as well as a desire for revenge. Given the vast resources of his enemies, the colonel was lucky to get off so lightly.

Bill Preston may not be so lucky. Constantine wants the house in Mykonos to give to his son (married to a daughter of Kakridis). Bill is trying to stop him, and even though he's paying a first-class lawyer I don't fancy his chances. He's a foreigner, with the full weight of the Greek establishment against him.

As for my case, the one against 'Ernest Hemingway', I've decided to drop all charges. The adventure of the past three months has opened my eyes. I was wasting my money and time. The guy is a well known liar and conman. I don't need to prove that in court.

Rosa Corneille continues to see auras, even in the bright sun of high summer. She tells me, in confidence, that Constantine Petrakis is unwell. His aura is 'kaput' and the rest will inevitably follow. Please don't repeat this to anyone, but it will be interesting to see if events bear out her beliefs. Stranger things have proved true, against all rational expectation.

Stelios Tasakos is being held by police and undergoing

psychological investigation. They are, apparently, looking after him with surprising tact and benevolence. His father seems to have a great burden off his mind. It can't be pleasant to have your son in the care of police psychiatrists, but if the young man is crazy that's a whole lot better than looking after him yourself. Perhaps by letting the light of acknowledgement into that miserable house, some of its darkness may disperse. It's a shame poor John Petrakis had to die for the cleansing to begin.

The colonel, meanwhile, is attempting to donate his house, including his library and art collection, to the state. His friends – led by me – are doing their best to dissuade him, since the state will not look after it. The house will simply be locked up and left to rot. The alternative is almost as bad: his son and daughter inherit, are forced to sell it to pay for tax, and the collection will be broken up. I am trying to put together a 'third way', by which he sets up a private foundation. With the colonel, however, it is always two steps forward, followed very quickly by two steps back. He agrees, then forgets he has agreed, and we start again from square one. If you hear that one (or both) of us has been committed to an asylum, don't be surprised.

I hope your experiences in Aegina were not so unpleasant as to prevent you returning for a visit. Each sunset, in my philosophy, is an opportunity for a drink, each drink a chance to adjust our minds to the troublesome kaleidoscope of life. You have my number and I hope you'll use it.

You did a good job. Be glad of that.
Abbas